KASSY O'ROARKE

GEOCACHER

KASSY O'ROARKE

GEOCACHER

PET DETECTIVE MYSTERIES
BOOK THREE

KELLY OLIVER

—Beaver's Pond Press—
Minneapolis, MN

PRAISE FOR
THE PET DETECTIVE MYSTERY SERIES

"A juicy middle-grade mystery in which a young investigator learns that it's okay to be vulnerable."

—*Foreword Reviews*

"A polished, convincing, kid-centered adventure, with endearing characters and a strong sense of middle-school humor. Oliver writes in a breezy, kid-friendly style that's perfect for early middle schoolers, who will easily identify with Kassy. A strong series debut!"

—*BlueInk Review*

"An action-packed and exciting adventure mystery novel. *Kassy O'Roarke, Cub Reporter* is well-written and likely to entertain both animal and mystery lovers of all ages. It's most highly recommended!"

—Jeff Mangus, *Readers' Favorite*

"Where was Kassy when I was growing up? With jokes, riddles, puzzles, and mysteries for readers to solve, this series is sure to provide hours of entertainment. These books will hone reasoning skills while also being lots of fun. I highly recommend this collection for any budding sleuth!"

—Claire Katz, director of the Philosophy for Children Texas Program and the Philosophy Camp for Teens and Tweens

"A whole lot of fun—and delivers in every way an adventure story should! The mystery's twists and turns are clever and unpredictable, but Kelly Oliver builds more than a detailed mystery. She also creates a heartwarming world populated with believable characters who feel like people you know."

—Sarah Scheele, *Readers' Favorite*

"Great fun, with its underpants-wearing animals and many memorable characters, like Flatulent Freddie the farting ferret. The book is action-packed, and the characters are all likable and realistic, with relatable problems. The plot has twists and turns that are sure to keep readers on their toes. I was hooked by the first page!"

—Kristen Van Campen (teen reviewer), *Readers' Favorite*

"This is a purely enjoyable adventure filled with memorable characters, an endearing protagonist, and a lot of heart."

—US Review of Books

"For everyone who's into adventure, mystery, and a whole bunch of middle-grade fun, this first in series does the trick! Beware, you won't want to set this book down anytime soon."

—Chanticleer Reviews

"Even more exciting than *The Mysterious Benedict Society*! The mysteries make you feel like you're really inside the adventure, with many fun animals and twists. These are excellent books for young journalists and detectives!"

—Mila Neely, fan review

Edited by Paige Polinsky
Illustrated by BNP Design Studio
Production editor: Hanna Kjeldbjerg
Cover illustration by BNP Design Studio

ISBN 13: 978-1-64343-821-4
Library of Congress Catalog Number: 2020922092
Printed in the United States of America
First Printing: 2021
25 24 23 22 21   5 4 3 2 1

Book design by Athena Currier

Beaver's Pond Press
939 West Seventh Street
Saint Paul, MN 55402
(952) 829-8818
www.BeaversPondPress.com

To order, visit www.kellyoliverbooks.com. Reseller discounts available.

For media inquiries, please call or e-mail Kelly Oliver at kellyoliverbooks@gmail.com.
For more information, visit www.kellyoliverbooks.com.

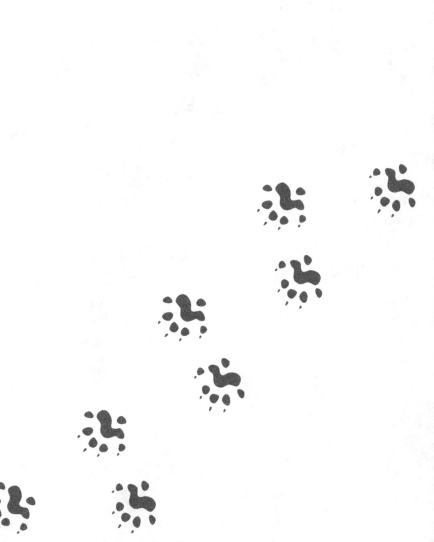

1

THE CONTEST

THOSE OF YOU WHO KNOW MY LITTLE BROTHER, Crispy, know he doesn't go anywhere without his pet ferret, flatulent Freddie. So, of course Freddie is in here stinking up our tent. But that's not the worst of it. Crispy also insisted on bringing our new miniature goat, Han Solo. Han smells even worse than Freddie. Who ever heard of a goat on a camping trip? Luckily, our golden retriever, Zeus, is sleeping in the RV with Dad and Mari.

It's bad enough my *sort-of* stepsister, Ronny, bounces her soccer ball off the walls of the tent and her little dog, Yara, snores. But a goat nibbling on my sleeping bag really takes the cake. Last night, after he finished gnawing on my sleeping bag, Han Solo ate my toothpaste for dessert . . . the whole tube.

Good thing Mom insists on organic Earthpaste made of clay, or we would have one very sick little goat.

In another three days, on lucky July 13, I'll be thirteen, so I don't see why I have to share a tent with these little hooligans. After all, I'm not a little kid anymore, not like Crispy, who's eight.

"Hey, whatcha doing?" Crispy asks. Freddie is wrapped around his neck, as usual.

"I'm writing in my new diary, if you must know." I'm keeping a journal of our adventures on the way to Washington, DC, so I can write about it for the school newspaper and submit a story when school starts up again. Mom got me this cool green diary so I can keep notes for my newspaper stories. I'm a journalist . . . and a pet detective.

"Can I watch?" he asks.

"Writing isn't a spectator sport." I push Han Solo away. "Knock it off." Now he's trying to eat my diary.

As some of you know, my name is Kassy O'Roarke. I find missing pets and then write articles about my cases for the school paper. Okay, so far, I've only written one story about our missing cougar cub, Apollo. But someday, I'll have my own column. If I can write a super good story, maybe I can make the front page yet. That's my goal in life, to be a front-page reporter—and a famous pet detective, of course.

"Whatcha writing about?" Crispy asks.

"About how you and Freddie smell like stinky cheese wrapped in dirty socks."

Freddie squeaks in protest.

"Why don't you write about how we're delivering Kiki to the National Zoo?"

Kiki is the koala bear charm we found while geocaching in Slug's front yard. Ronny put the charm on a bracelet. (Never mind about Slug. He's grounded back home in Lemontree Heights, Tennessee.) She was hidden inside a purple plastic Easter egg, along with a note:

Kiki the koala started her journey in Canberra, Australia. She has always wanted to visit her relatives in the Smithsonian National Zoo. Help her get to Washington!

So, what is geocaching, you ask? It's an outdoor game like a treasure hunt. People hide stuff and upload the coordinates to the Internet. Then other people go search for it and report their findings. Kiki is a travel bug—that's the lingo for a cache that travels. Different people find it and hide it in new places, over and over again.

Ronny's really into it. Even though she's only ten, Ronny has a cell phone and I don't. Mom is a Luddite—that's someone who doesn't believe in technology. I mean, she uses computers and cell phones herself, but she won't let me have them. She says they'll rot my brain. Instead, she believes in the great outdoors, which is why I was allowed to go on this camping trip with my dad and his girlfriend, Mari. I think Mom is just trying to get Crispy and me out of her hair for a while.

Back to geocaching and Rotten Ronny. She says you log all the info about the travel bug in a geocaching app. I wouldn't know because you need a cell phone or a computer or a GPS to play. And I don't have any of those. So, the only way I can find caches is to follow Rotten Ronny, and she goes so fast that she's pretty hard to keep up with.

It's hard to imagine someone carried Kiki halfway around the globe. Now we're on a mission to get her to the zoo. My dad had already planned to take us camping in Shenandoah National Park in Virginia, and my brainy little brother pointed out that it's only another hour and a half from there to DC. Of all the folks who've carried Kiki, we will be the ones to deliver her to her destination.

Shenandoah Park is pretty nice. There are hiking trails, creeks, and caves with my least favorite creatures on earth— bats. At night, they fly out of the caves and swoop down from the trees. *Disgusting.* And there are so many trees here. I've never seen so many trees.

After breakfast, I'm sitting under a giant oak, writing in my journal. The campground is full. Some kids are riding their bikes around on the paved roads, and a family of four is cooking hot dogs over a campfire. Another group of kids is heading out to the river to go fishing. Crispy, Freddie, and Han Solo are sitting next to me, watching me write, which is kind of distracting. And Ronny is kicking her soccer ball all around the campground.

Speak of the deviled egg. The ball whizzes at my face, but Ronny blocks it just in the nick of time. I scowl. This morning, she wouldn't come out of our tent because her shirt was wrinkled, and now she's kicking a dirty ball all over the place. At least she's kicking it outside the tent.

"Hey, Kassy," she pants. "Have you seen this?" She holds up a flyer.

"What is it?"

Ronny kneels down beside me and shoves the flyer in my face. "A geocaching treasure hunt."

I snag the flyer out of her hand and read it.

Join Camp Shenandoah for a geocaching treasure hunt this Saturday and Sunday. Riddles, prizes, and fun!

"Riddles!" Crispy says, reading over my shoulder. He loves riddles. "I bet we could win."

"Let's do it," Ronny says, bouncing her ball from knee to knee. She's even given her soccer ball a name, Xavier, after some famous soccer player.

"Interesting idea." I turn the flyer over to read the rules.

---

1. **All contestants/teams must sign up by 5:00 p.m. Friday.**

2. **All contestants/teams meet at the Nature Center on Saturday at 9:00 a.m. Contest ends at noon on Sunday.**

Saturday—that's tomorrow. But we have to register by 5:00 p.m. today.

"Crispy's right," Ronny says. "I bet we could win."

"I wonder what the prizes are," Crispy says, scratching Freddie behind the ears. The ferret chirps. "Freddie hopes they're dog biscuits."

"First place gets a new tent," I read. *Chicken-fried steak!* A new tent. *Wow.* I could have peace and quiet to read and write my articles for the school newspaper. My own tent.

Maybe they're right. With Crispy's talent for riddles, Ronny's experience geocaching, and my detective skills, we just might have a chance.

I fold the flyer and slip it into a pocket of my spy vest. I call it my spy vest, but it's really just one of Dad's old fishing vests with tons of pockets. In my vest, I keep my magnifying glass, string, tape, my notebook and pencil, a couple of emergency granola bars, a piece of jerky, and some dog biscuits. You never know when you might end up trapped in some stinky old shed or lost in the woods or something and need a snack. The granola bars, not the dog biscuits—those are to bribe missing dogs.

Han Solo nibbles at my pocket. He's probably after the granola bars . . . or the paper. Or the string. Han Solo will eat just about anything—he's a goat, after all. Once he even ate a

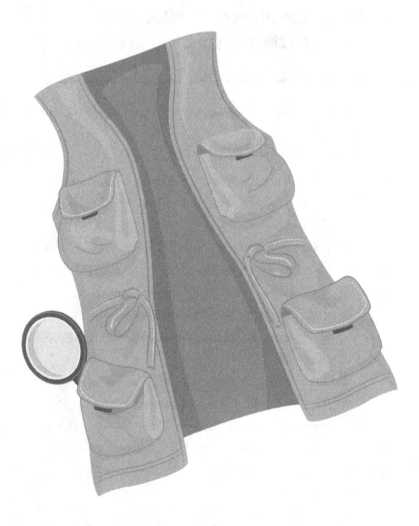

pair of my dad's droopy underpants. You have to watch him like a hawk or he'll eat the shoes off your feet. Back home at our petting zoo, he always samples everyone else's dinner. He'll eat Chewy the chimp's bananas, but being an herbivore, he draws the line at Apollo the cougar cub's raw steak dinner.

Freddie the ferret, on the other hand, is a strict carnivore and eats only meat, which is why Mom told Crispy to put Freddie on a diet. No more cookies for him. Technically, I'm an omnivore, which means I eat everything. Mom says I'm a picky eater . . . but that's because she tries to sneak zucchini and other green vegetables into her gluten-free baked goods. I hate zucchini almost as much as I hate bats.

"Lunchtime, kids," Mari calls from our campsite. It's weird being on a camping trip with Mari instead of Mom.

My stomach growls. No wonder I'm thinking of food. I'm starving. I stand up and brush the dirt off my butt. Ronny, Crispy, Freddie, and Han Solo follow me back over to our campsite. I wonder what's for lunch. Mari is from Cuba and likes to cook traditional Cuban dishes like rice and black beans and plantains. She's a way better cook than Mom. That's one point in her favor.

Don't tell Mom, but the gluten-free sugar cookies *made out of vegetables* she sent with us for the trip are rumbling around in Han Solo's round tummy. At least someone likes Mom's cooking.

"Hey, guys. Ready for some chow?" Dad is all smiles. He's probably just glad to be away from his law office. "I cooked lunch." He's standing over a smoking barbecue. "Burgers—and a veggie burger for Percy." My brother, Crispy, is an herbivore, which basically means he's a vegetarian. He refuses to eat his animal friends. Maybe that's why he gets along so well with our camel, Spittoon. Luckily, we left him at home at the petting zoo, but only because he wouldn't fit in the RV. If Crispy had his way, the whole zoo would be camping with us.

Yeah, my little brother's real name is Percy. I call him Crispy because he almost burned down our barn a year ago.

"Dig in," Dad says, passing out paper plates.

"Daddy, can we enter the geocaching treasure hunt?" Ronny asks. Yeah, she calls *my* father *Daddy*, which really gets my goat. "It's tomorrow and Sunday."

"I don't know, honey." He takes a big bite of burger. "We're leaving tomorrow morning."

"But, Dad . . ." Crispy chimes in.

"Sorry, kiddo, but we only have the campsite reserved for tonight." Dad reaches over and ruffles Crispy's hair.

Brussels sprouts! No new tent for me. I drop my burger back onto my plate. I'm not hungry anymore.

2

KIKI GOES MISSING

I CHECK MY SPY WATCH. It's quarter to five, the deadline to register for the treasure hunt. Even though we're leaving tomorrow, it doesn't hurt to go check it out, right? Just out of curiosity . . .

I drag Crispy and Ronny over to the Nature Center to check out the competition. At least we can size up the other contestants. Who knows, maybe we can persuade Dad to let us stay here until Sunday. I'm imagining myself in my own private tent writing the next front-page story for the newspaper without a goat eating my hair or a ferret farting in my face.

The Nature Center is a log cabin at the far end of the campground. Inside, there are displays explaining the flora and fauna native to Shenandoah National Park. A plaque at the entrance says the park hosts over 1,400 plant species, with everything from mosses and liverworts to lichens and fungi. And there are over 50 different species of mammals, including black bears, white-tailed deer, woodchucks, chipmunks, beavers, raccoons, and my nemesis: *Eptesicus fuscus*, the big brown bat.

I count ten other kids milling around, checking out the exhibits. A few are gathered around a stuffed *Rattus rattus*, otherwise known as a black rat. I wander over and join them.

"It's so cute," says one pig-tailed little girl. She leans in to get a closer look. "I love its tiny ears." She probably thinks bats are cute too. Although I have to admit, rats are super smart, and at least they don't fly into your hair and scare you half to death.

I read the sign on the wall next to the exhibit.

The black rat (*Rattus rattus*) is also known as ship rat, roof rat, and house rat. Farmers consider it a pest because it eats a wide range of crops. Sometimes it is kept as a pet.

Great. Now Crispy will want a rat. And in parts of India, it is considered sacred. Pest, pet, or providence? As Mom says, to each their own.

"Attention." A forest ranger appears out of nowhere and starts tapping a pencil against a desk. She's wearing a khaki uniform and a big Smokey Bear hat. "Children, can I get your attention, please?" She drops the pencil and claps her hands together. "Kids, listen up." She keeps clapping until all heads turn and all eyes are on her. "Ready for some fun?"

"Yes," we all say.

"I didn't hear you."

"*Yes!*"

She holds up a box. "Do y'all want to win this new tent?"

"Yes."

"I can't hear you."

"*Yes!*"

"How about ribbons? Who wants to win a ribbon?"

"Me! Me!" Most of the kids raise their hands, including Ronny and Crispy.

I cross my arms over my chest and roll my eyes. *Can we please just get on with it?*

"Let's start with introductions. I'm Ranger Judy." The ranger scans the room. "Redheads, why don't you go first." She points in my direction.

I hate it when people identify me by my hair. At least she didn't call me Ginger, or Red, or Carrot Top. I look around to see if there are any other redheads in my vicinity.

"I'm Percy O'Roarke," Crispy pipes up. He has red hair too and doesn't seem to care what people call him. "And these are my sisters, Ronny and Kassy." *Oh, so now Ronny has been promoted to "sister" and she gets top billing?*

"And what brings the O'Roarkes to Shenandoah National Park?" Ranger Judy asks with a smile.

"We're taking Kiki to the zoo in Washington," Ronny says. She pulls the silver koala bear charm from her pocket and holds it up. "We found this travel bug in Tennessee, but it came all the way from Australia."

"Wow, travel bugs are so fun," the pig-tailed girl says. "What a cute bear. Can I see it?" Her glasses are even thicker than mine. And she has good taste. She's wearing a Hello Kitty shirt. She's smaller than Crispy, so she must be about six or seven.

Reluctantly, Ronny hands it over.

"The O'Roarkes from Tennessee." Ranger Judy writes on her clipboard. "And what about y'all?"

She points to three kids in front of the snake exhibit. They're huddled together, giggling. *What's so funny about snakes?*

"What are your names, and what brings you to the park?" the ranger asks.

The tallest one has slicked-back hair and cowboy boots. "We're the Cheevers," he says. "I'm Derek, and this is my sister, Bethany, and my brother, Kaboom, and we're going to win this contest." He pumps the air with his fist, and his siblings join him. "We're from West Virginia, the greatest state in the union."

The Cheevers look more like beavers. They all have big front teeth and dark, beady eyes. Derek has a leather knife holster hanging from his belt. Bethany's wearing a fringe jacket and big black army boots. She looks a little older than I am. And Kaboom is sporting a crew cut and has sports glasses wrapped around his head with an elastic band. He's about Ronny's age, maybe ten or eleven. They're still cheering and fist pumping.

They're so hyped up that I wonder if they ate too much ice cream for lunch.

"We've got the O'Roarkes and the Cheevers! Who's next?" Ranger Judy asks.

"Me," the pig-tailed girl says. "I'm Gabby, and this is my brother, Marco."

Marco is playing a game on his phone and doesn't look up. His wavy hair flops over his eyes. He's wearing a T-shirt with a lightning bolt and the words *Ride the Lightning*. Must be the name of some heavy metal band.

"And your last name?" the ranger asks.

"Gonzalez." Now Marco looks up from his phone and silently stares at a stuffed lynx. "We're from Michigan."

Ranger Judy writes on her clipboard. "And what about y'all?" She gestures toward the last group, a team of five.

They look at each other. Finally, one of them says, "We're cousins. My sisters and I live in Massachusetts, and our cousins live in New York." The kid is tall with long brown hair and a rainbow T-shirt. "My name is Ky Johnson, I'm fourteen, and just so you know, my pronouns are *they/them*." With their long neck, Ky reminds me of a giraffe.

"Can I get the rest of y'all's names?"

Ky has two younger sisters around my age, Kaleigh and Kristy. They both have long blond hair and matching pink shirts. Maybe they're twins. The way they're braiding each other's hair reminds me of blond capuchin monkeys grooming each other.

Their cousins are Jimmy and Bobby Marino from Long Island, New York. Jimmy and Bobby are fighting over

something near the salamander exhibit. Ky tells them to knock it off.

"Great," Ranger Judy says. "We have four teams for the contest."

I don't bother to tell her we're not staying.

She passes out colored name tags with pictures of animals on them. "The O'Roarkes will be Team Golden Eagle." As she hands Crispy his name tag, Freddie stretches out to his full length and reaches for the key ring attached to her belt.

"Freddie likes to steal keys," Crispy says.

The ranger laughs and swats at the ferret. "Well, he won't get mine." She ducks out of Freddie's reach and heads toward the snake exhibit. "The Cheevers will be Team Red Fox."

"Go Foxes! Yeah!" Derek shouts.

Kaboom joins in. "Go Foxes. Let's win!"

I think Ranger Judy should rename them the Eager Beavers.

"The Gonzalezes will be Team Blue Heron." She hands them blue name tags with herons on them.

Gabby twists her pigtail and asks, "What's a blue heron?"

"A large wading bird in the family Ardeidae," Crispy says.

Gabby turns the tag over in her little hand. "I don't want to be an ugly bird."

Ranger Judy sorts through her stack of name tags. "How about a white-tailed deer? Would you rather be a deer?"

"Can I see it?" Gabby asks.

The ranger hands her a white name tag with a picture of a deer on it.

"Okay. Deers are cute. I like deers." Through her thick glasses, her brown eyes look as big as a deer's.

"Deer," Ranger Judy corrects her. "The plural of *deer* is just *deer*."

Gabby looks confused.

"Like moose," Crispy chimes in. "You don't say *mooses*."

Gabby scrunches her eyebrows, then starts to peel the waxy paper off the back of the name tag.

"Not so fast," the ranger says. She hands Gabby a big black marker. "Pass this around. Everyone, write your name on your tag and put it on tomorrow morning."

"What about us?" Bobby Marino asks. "We don't have name tags yet. What are we?"

"Right." Ranger Judy walks over to the salamander exhibit. "Last but not least, the Johnsons-Marinos will be Team Brown Bear."

Jimmy and Bobby kind of look like bears. They're both big and burly like junior high football players. Bobby has a round, freckly face. It's hard to believe those grizzlies are related to Ky and their sisters. Funny how people in the same family can be so different from each other. Mom chalks it up to genetic mutations. Dad just says, "Variety is the spice of life."

"Listen up, teams. Here are the rules." Ranger Judy passes out another sheet of paper to each team. She reads from the sheet: "Teams must put the cache back exactly where they found it. Teams should take only their token from each cache. The first team to collect their tokens from all eight caches wins the grand prize." She glances around the room. "Any questions?"

"What if there's a tie?" Gabby asks.

Ranger Judy gets a puzzled look on her face. "We'll cross that bridge when we come to it. If any team needs a GPS, you can have your parents come to the center and check one out. But this isn't a regular old geocache. This is a puzzle-and-riddle cache, so you'll have to rely on your wits more than your gear."

Whew. Good thing. I've never geocached before, and I don't know how to use a GPS . . . but I *have* had to use my wits to solve missing pet cases. How different can this be?

"We start at 0900 hours tomorrow," Ranger Judy says, pointing at the clock above her desk.

"That means nine in the morning," Crispy chimes in.

"Very good," the ranger says. "Meet right here. Are there any questions?"

Gabby points at Crispy. "What's that animal around his neck? It's so-o-o cute." She holds her nose. "But it stinks! Is it a weasel?"

"Freddie is *Mustela putorius furo*," Crispy says. "A domesticated polecat in the same genus as the weasel. Like skunks, they release anal gland secretions when scared." Crispy turns his head to kiss Freddie on the nose. "Right, little guy? Is she scaring you?"

When Crispy says *anal gland*, everyone starts giggling.

"And he farts too!" Ronny shouts above the laughter.

Crispy pouts. "He can't help it. Anyway, Mom says it's natural to pass gas."

The laughter gets louder, and I want to crawl into a hole. *Why can't my brainiac brother and his stinky ferret just blend in like other kids and their pets?*

"Settle down," Ranger Judy says. "You'll get your first clue tomorrow morning. In the meantime, rest up and get ready for some serious fun!" She disappears into a back office.

"Can I pet him?" Gabby moves closer to Freddie and holds out her hand.

Crispy pulls Freddie down from around his neck. "Sure. He likes to be scratched under the chin. See?"

"Does he bite?"

Crispy shakes his head. "Not usually."

Slowly, Gabby touches Freddie. "Ooh. He's so soft." She smiles up at my brother. "Can I hold him?"

Crispy shows her how. "Hold him under his arms, like this. And watch out for his claws. They're nonretractable."

"What's that mean?"

"His claws stick out. Not like a cat that can pull its claws back in."

"Oh, okay." Gabby reaches for Freddie. The ferret squirms out of her grasp and climbs back up on my brother's shoulder.

"He's shy," Crispy says, petting Freddie's head.

"Like my brother." Gabby looks around for Marco. He's still staring at the stuffed lynx.

Derek Cheever smirks at us on the way out the door. "Watch out that your stinky rat doesn't get eaten by a fox."

Kaboom is right behind his big brother. "Yeah, the foxes will eat your lunch," he says with a grin.

"He's not a rat!" Crispy yells after them.

"We should go," I say. "Dad and Mari will be wondering where we went."

"See you tomorrow." Gabby waves.

I wish. Now I really want to enter this contest. I especially want to show those eager-beaver Cheevers a thing or two. But Dad won't budge.

"Guess I won't be needing this." I set my name tag on a table by the door. "Come on. Let's go." We're the last ones to leave.

Ronny tucks Xavier under her arm and picks up my name tag. "I hope we can stay."

"Me too." I hold the door open for her. "Oh well. At least we'll get Kiki to the National Zoo."

Ronny gets a weird look on her face. She pats the pockets of her shorts.

"Where is Kiki?"

"Don't you have her?" Ronny's eyes are wide.

"No. Maybe Crispy does." I go back inside to fetch Crispy, who is showing Freddie his "cousins" at the weasel exhibit.

"Hey, Crispy, do you have Kiki?"

"Kiki? No." Crispy pulls a piece of kibble from his pants pocket and feeds it to Freddie. "Why? Is she missing?"

"Either Kiki is lying around somewhere or one of the other kids pocketed her." I scan the floor. "Help me look for her."

Crispy, Ronny, and I search the Nature Center from top to bottom. No sign of Kiki.

"We've got to find her!" Ronny has tears in her eyes. "We can't leave without Kiki." Ronny's so upset that she's hyperventilating. That's like panting for humans.

"You're a pet detective," Crispy says. "If anyone can find Kiki, you can."

"You're right." This counts as an emergency, so I pull an emergency granola bar from my pocket, unwrap it, and take a bite. "Now we *have* to stay. But how will we convince Dad?"

3

FLAT TIRES

THE NEXT MORNING, DAD SHAKES OUR TENT. "Rise and shine, sleepyheads. We've got to hit the road."

Pickled beets. I can tell even without looking outside that it's still dark. I roll over and groan. Who gets up before the sun?

Han Solo pulls on my hair with his teeth. *Geez.* He must be working for Dad. *I'd better get up before he gives me a haircut.*

Even with the goat chomping around inside the tent and Dad rattling outside it, Crispy, Freddie, and Ronny are still sound asleep. I'm sandwiched in between them in my sleeping bag. Crispy's sleeping-bag-encased feet are on top of mine. I move my legs out from under his and reach out to nudge him. Freddie is curled up on top of my brother's head. He opens his

24

beady little eyes and stares up at me as if to say, "Don't touch my human." I retract my hand.

"Okay, ferret, have it your way." I scooch out of my sleeping bag and sit up. My head almost touches the top of the tent, and I'm still pinned between Crispy and Ronny.

On hands and knees, I crawl to the tent door and unzip it. Wake-up call. Cool, fresh air hits my cheeks. Smells like food. Mari must be cooking breakfast already. *Who eats at this hour?* I press a button on my spy watch and its face lights up. Five in the morning. *Whoa.* Dad really is determined to make an early

start. He always says, "The early bird gets the worm." Worms are overrated.

No matter how much we begged to stay, he said, "No can do." *How can he just leave Kiki here? How can we abandon our mission to get her to the National Zoo? And what about the contest? It's just two more measly days . . . We're on vacation, so what's the hurry?* I keep my questions to myself. I know from experience pestering Dad will just make it worse.

"Hey, kiddo. Get your little brother and sister up, okay?" Dad is setting paper plates out on the picnic table by the light of a battery-operated lantern.

"Can I go pee first?" I hold up my toothbrush. "And brush my teeth?"

"Here, take this." He holds out a flashlight.

"Thanks, but I already have one." I pat my spy vest. Now I even wear it to bed, especially when sleeping out in the wilderness.

"Okay. But be careful." Dad goes back to setting the table.

As I trudge over to the bathroom, I brainstorm arguments to appeal to Dad's lawyerly side. As a lawyer, he appreciates rational arguments.

This campground is kind of creepy in the dark. Our tent is the farthest from the bathrooms, of course. And we're completely surrounded by trees. Now I wish I'd taken Dad's big flashlight . . . My pocket flashlight looks like a stray firefly.

A noise startles me, and I drop my flashlight. *Brussels sprouts!* I freeze and tighten my grip on my toothbrush. "Who's there?" I call into the darkness. Bushes rustle behind me, and I whip around. I hold my breath and listen. *Is it a bear? Or a cougar?* Between the two, I'm hoping bear. At least most bears are *generally* herbivores, unless you count ants and termites.

Don't panic, I tell myself. *Keep calm. And whatever you do, don't run.* Cougars and grizzlies love to chase their prey. I remind myself that there are no grizzlies in Shenandoah National Park. But there are black bears! *Look big and scary.* Wielding my toothbrush, I put both arms in the air and growl as loud as I can. The rustling stops . . . and a squirrel runs past me.

Whew! How can such a small animal make such a big noise?

"Kassandra, what in the world are you doing?"

I nearly jump out of my skin. Mari appears on the path, holding the big flashlight.

"Mari, you scared me. Don't sneak up on me like that."

"Where are you going in the dark by yourself?" Mari puts her arm around my shoulders. "Breakfast is ready." "Will you come to the bathroom with me?" I'm embarrassed to ask. I mean, I'm almost thirteen and afraid to go to the bathroom by myself? *Come on, Kassy, get a grip.*

"Sure, *mijita.*" She shines the light on the path.

"I lost my flashlight." I glance around, hoping to find it.

"We'll get it later," Mari says. "Let's do one thing at a time. Bathroom, then breakfast."

By the time Mari escorts me to the bathroom and then back to our camp, everyone is sitting at the picnic table. Crispy is feeding Freddie bits of pancake soaked in syrup. I'm so shook up, I don't remind him that Mom put Freddie on a diet. All those cookies and sweets aren't good for a ferret. And Freddie is getting fat. Han Solo is standing with his little hooves on the picnic table bench, begging for a pancake. And Ronny is talking with her mouth full . . . something Mom doesn't allow me to do at home. Then again, Ronny gets to do lots of things I don't. Like talk on her cell phone and surf the Internet.

In the middle of our breakfast, the sunrise turns the sky the color of orange sherbet. A chorus of birdsong fills the air with the sounds of morning, and the sweet smells of the forest float on the evaporating dew. It's so pretty. I should describe it in my journal for my article: "Life in the Shenandoah Forest."

"What the—" Dad bursts out and jumps up. He's staring over my shoulder.

I crank my head around to see what he's looking at. *Holy hoodwink!* Both the front and the rear tires on our rented RV are flat.

Dad grabs the flashlight and runs around to the other side of the RV.

I follow him. Yup. All the tires are flat. *Whoa. Did someone slash our tires?*

"I guess we're not going anywhere." Dad sighs and runs his hand through his hair. He does that when he's upset.

Who would want to slash our tires? Someone who wants to keep us here. I return to the picnic table. Crispy and Ronny are showing each other the doughy contents of their mouths, giggling like hyenas. *Disgusting*.

"All the tires are flat," I announce as I slide onto the bench next to my brother. "Now we have to stay."

"Really?" Crispy swallows his mouthful.

"Hooray!" Ronny bounces Xavier off the edge of the table, then jumps up and dribbles it with her head. "Now we can find Kiki and win the contest."

I squint at the two hoodlums. "Did one of you do it?"

"Do what?" they ask in unison.

"Flatten the tires."

They look at me like I'm speaking Klingon. Although, I'm sure Crispy is fluent in Klingon. That's the kind of nerdy kid he is.

"No way." Ronny stops dribbling and clutches her ball. "Why would we flatten our own tires?"

I raise my eyebrows. *Isn't it obvious?*

"Well, I guess you kiddos will be geocaching after all." Dad comes back to the table and grabs a paper towel to wipe off his dirty hands. "We only have one spare. I called the RV place, but they're closed until Monday."

Ronny jumps up and down. "Hooray!" When Crispy joins her jumping like a kangaroo, Freddie toots in protest.

Phew. I fan my hand in front of my nose.

"I thought that would make you happy." Dad plops down at the picnic table. "Might as well enjoy it." He helps himself to more pancakes. "There are worse places to be stuck." He pats the bench next to him, and Mari takes a seat. When he kisses her on the cheek, I turn the other way.

I still think he should be kissing Mom instead. Mom says when I grow up, then I'll understand. But I don't think I ever will.

Since we still have an hour before the contest starts, I'm watching Dad mess around with the tires. He's pouring soapy water over them.

"Did someone let the air out?" Crispy asks.

"It's pretty tricky to let the air out of these tires," Dad says. "You'd have to remove this cap." He holds up the small black cap. "And then depress this." He points to a tiny metal post inside the air valve. "You'd need a tool, and it would take a while." He squats down next to the back tire and douses it with soapy water. "Aha!"

"Whatcha doing?" Ronny asks.

"See where the tire is bubbling?"

"Yeah."

"Well, that means air is getting out in that spot. There's a small hole."

"But how?" I ask. Someone must have put it there. I mean, what are the chances all six tires would deflate at the same time?

"We might have run over a nail or a sharp piece of glass on our way in . . ."

"You mean *four* nails or *four* sharp pieces of glass." I squat down next to him and examine the back tire. It's definitely bubbling out of a spot near the top. When I lean closer, I see a small slit.

"Seems suspicious, doesn't it?" Dad says. "I've seen some teenage hooligans running around. You don't think one of them pulled this stunt, do you?"

I think of Derek Cheever—and the knife hanging from his belt. "Why would they do that?"

"Who knows?" Dad shakes his head. "Well, you kiddos had better get over to the Nature Center if you're going to win that geo-contest thing."

I check my spy watch. He's right. It's nearly nine. We've been goofing off with the tires for almost an hour. "You guys ready to win a new tent?" I ask.

"Yes!" Crispy and Ronny sing in unison.

"Let's do it." I pump my fist in the air, imitating Derek Cheever. I pat my trusty spy vest, and we head for the Nature Center.

On the way, a little voice comes from behind us. "Guys, guys, wait up. Guess what?"

I turn around. It's pig-tailed Gabby with Marco in tow. "What?" I play along.

She holds out a tooth in the palm of her hand. "My tooth fell out. I'm going to put it under my pillow for the tooth fairy."

"Cool," I say. Must be nice to believe in childish fantasies. I don't want to burst her bubble by telling her the tooth fairy isn't real.

"Can I touch it?" Ronny asks.

Gross.

I ignore them and start walking. "Only ten minutes until showtime," I call out. "Better get a move on, slowpokes."

The Cheevers (a.k.a. the Red Foxes), are first in line outside the Nature Center. I'm guessing the door's still locked. Behind them are the Brown Bears: Ky, Kaleigh, Kristy, and their rowdy cousins Bobby and Jimmy. We fall in line behind the Brown Bears, and Gabby and Marco—the White-Tailed Deer—line up behind us. Ky is examining a leaf under a magnifying glass. Kaleigh and Kristy are looking at something on a cell phone. Bobby and Jimmy are poking each other. Marco is staring off into space. Gabby is chatting up Ronny.

I remove the backing from my name tag and attach it to my shirt. Ronny and Crispy do the same. I glance at my spy watch. Nine on the dot. Where's Ranger Judy?

I've got my spy vest loaded with tools of the trade. Ronny's got her cell phone and, of course, Xavier. What good is a soccer ball for geocaching, you ask? You haven't seen Ronny kick a soccer ball.

Then there's Crispy and Freddie. Crispy's got his talent with riddles. And Freddie's got . . . well, let's just say Freddie has his own not-so-secret weapon.

The Golden Eagles are ready for action.

4
THE GOLDEN EAGLES

AS RANGER JUDY REMINDS US OF THE RULES of the contest, excitement fills the room. No one can stand still. We're all so eager to get started.

The other kids poke at their siblings, laugh, and squirm around. I observe them, trying to determine who might have taken Kiki. It's going to take all my detective skills and more to find her. Whoever took her didn't leave me any obvious clues.

"Settle down," Ranger Judy says. "There is an animal token in each cache matching your team mascot: an eagle, a bear, a deer, and a fox. When you find the first cache, take your team's token and bring it back here, where you'll trade the token for the next clue in the treasure hunt."

Bobby and Jimmy are feeding the stuffed lynx a string of black licorice and kicking at each other with their high-top tennis shoes.

"Boys, please don't touch the exhibits," the ranger says. "Each team must stay together at all times. You will all be searching for different caches, so you can't just follow another team to find the cache."

I raise my hand.

"You have a question?" She points to me. "Kassy of the Golden Eagles. Shoot."

"So each team is doing its own geocache? Then why are there tokens for each team?"

"Good question. You will all search for the same caches but at different times. So you're not all racing to the same cache at once; I'll give a different clue to each team when they return to trade in their tokens. By the end of the hunt, every team will have found all the same caches. Does that make sense?"

"What if we want to keep our animal tokens?" Gabby asks.

"You can keep one after the contest is over. But to get the next clue, you have to turn in your token." Ranger Judy holds up something that looks like a small walkie-talkie. "Did every team get a GPS device? If not, you can still have your parents sign one out."

Crispy, Ronny, and I look at each other. "We don't," Ronny says. "But I have a cell phone."

"Here. Have your parents come by later to sign for it." The ranger hands a device to Ronny. "It doubles as a GPS and a walkie-talkie." She scans the room. "Everyone hold up your GPS devices."

All the team leaders hold up their devices.

"If you need anything, just push this button and ask for help," the ranger says. "I'll be able to hear you and track your coordinates. All the caches are within the campground or just a few feet into one of the trailheads. So I'll never be more than a few minutes away if you need me."

The ranger holds up a GPS. "Have you heard of longitude and latitude?" she asks. "They measure the whole circumference of the globe in degrees and minutes." She shows us how to operate the GPS to find the location of the caches in relation to our own position.

"Why is the earth measured in minutes?" I ask. "Aren't minutes a unit of time and measurement is about space?"

"Good question." The ranger smiles. "Both time and space are measured in minutes and seconds, both with sixty seconds in a minute."

Ronny hands the GPS to me. I stuff it into the giant pocket across the back of my vest.

"I can tell you that zero degrees longitude is called the prime meridian, and it's in Greenwich, England, and zero degrees latitude is the equator." Ranger Judy speaks into her walkie-talkie. "Hey, Frank, can you and Aisha come out here, please?"

A deep voice crackles back: "Ten-four."

A few seconds later, two more adults in khaki uniforms appear from the back office. Unlike Ranger Judy, they aren't wearing Smokey Bear hats. Instead, the man is wearing a tan baseball cap, and the woman is wearing a black head scarf.

"Kids, I want y'all to meet Ranger Frank and Ranger Aisha," Ranger Judy says. "They'll be circling the geocache course in case anyone needs help."

Ranger Frank and Ranger Aisha wave.

"Any other questions?"

"What about lunch?" Bobby Brown Bear asks.

"Good question. Your GPS device also has a clock. At noon, meet back here for lunch. We have a little picnic planned

for y'all. In the meantime . . . Ranger Aisha, can you pass out the snacks?"

Ranger Aisha disappears into the back office and returns a minute later with a big box. Like an airline flight attendant, she walks around passing out apples, granola bars, and peanut butter crackers. "Take whatever you want," she says.

Jimmy Brown Bear takes a handful of crackers and stuffs them into his backpack.

Ky's nose twitches as they move their hand back and forth over the box, trying to decide. They settle on an apple. Kaleigh and Kristy just shake their heads.

"You girls had better take something too," Ranger Aisha says. "In case you get hungry."

"We're okay," Kaleigh says. "We've got our own snacks." She holds up a bag of celery sticks.

Geez. You call that a snack?

Ranger Aisha offers the box to me.

"Can I have one of each?" I ask.

"Sure. Help yourself."

I take an apple, a granola bar, and some peanut butter crackers. I've learned from experience that it's always good to have snacks along. And since I ate my emergency granola bar yesterday, I need to restock.

"Can I have an extra granola bar for Freddie?" Crispy asks.

Ranger Aisha nods. "Of course." She pets Freddie on the head. "Hi there, little fella."

I scowl at Crispy and grab the granola bar out of his hand. "Freddie's on a diet, remember?"

Derek Cheever raises his hand.

"Yes, Derek of the Red Foxes. Do you have a question?"

"Can I have more snacks?" He wipes his mouth on his sleeve. "I just ate mine."

She scrunches her brows. "Didn't you get any breakfast?"

"Well, yeah. But I'm still hungry."

Ranger Aisha presents the box to the Cheevers again, and each of them takes another handful.

My stomach growls. When you get up before dawn, even pancakes can't get you through to lunchtime.

"Stock up, kids," Ranger Judy says. "It's going to be a busy morning. Does everyone have water?" She whispers something to Ranger Frank, who trots off to the back office. He comes back a minute later with a case of small water bottles.

"On your way out, I want everyone to take a bottle of water," Ranger Judy says. "It's important to stay hydrated. And if you get hungry or thirsty, just come back here and we'll take care of you. Any more questions?"

Everyone shakes their heads.

"Okay. Let's have some fun!"

The kids hoot and cheer. Derek Cheever shouts, "Go Team Red Fox!" and pumps his fist in the air.

"One more thing." Ranger Judy holds up a hand and raises her voice above the noise. "Very important. Everyone must report back here by five this afternoon. Got that? Hunting for caches after five isn't allowed or you'll be disqualified."

The Cheevers, Bobby, and Jimmy are still making noise. Gabby is talking to a stuffed racoon.

The ranger claps her hands together. "Can I have your attention, please?"

The noise dies down.

"Five o'clock. Everyone must be back here by five. Got it?"

"Got it," we repeat.

"Okay, here is your first clue." She passes out a different-colored index card to each team. "I'm appointing team leaders. Kassy, you'll be team leader for the Golden Eagles." She hands me a yellow card with a typed clue on it.

"Derek, you'll be team leader for the Red Foxes." She hands him a red index card.

"Gabby, you'll be team leader for the White-Tailed Deer." She hands Gabby a white index card.

She hands a tan index card to Ky. "And, Ky, you'll lead the Brown Bears."

Ranger Judy claps again. "Okay. Get out there—and most importantly, have fun!"

There's a rush for the door. I hang back, watching.

One of these kids took Kiki. But who would want a koala bear charm? Gabby said it was cute. Did she like it enough to keep it? Jimmy and Bobby might have kept it as some sort of practical joke. Derek Cheever would have kept it if he thought it was a competition. He's definitely set on winning. Maybe he wants to be the one to deliver Kiki to the National Zoo . . .

That gives me an idea. I need to find out if any of these families are heading to Washington. If they're mega-geocachers, maybe they couldn't resist taking a travel bug like Kiki.

"What are you waiting for?" Ronny asks. "Read the clue."

"Yeah, what does it say?" Crispy chimes in. "Should we get going?"

"We don't want to get trampled." I take out my notebook and pencil. "Anyway, I'm sizing up these kids to figure out who took Kiki."

"Do you have any suspects?" Crispy tries to see what I'm writing.

"Everyone is a suspect at this point."

"Even the forest rangers?" Ronny asks.

"Everyone." I hadn't thought of the adults. But I shouldn't rule them out. Maybe one of the rangers wants Kiki. I write *Forest Rangers?* in my notebook.

"Read the card!" Ronny is bouncing her soccer ball off her knee. "I want to look for the first cache."

Crispy grabs the card out of my hand. His lips move silently as he reads the clue.

"*Out loud!*" Ronny says. "What does it say?" She's jumping up and down, bouncing Xavier off the floor.

"The riddle is easy, but what does it mean?" Crispy asks, opening the door. Before he can step outside, the Cheevers come barreling in.

"We found it!" Kaboom says, holding up a fox token.

"Easy peasy." His sister, Bethany, does a little dance, her army boots kicking the air.

"No way you'll beat us," Derek says, glaring at me.

I tighten my lips.

He laughs. "I bet you haven't even started yet."

"You would win that bet," Crispy says, scowling at me.

Hey, it's not my fault. How did I know the Over-a-Cheevers would find the first cache so fast?

The Red Foxes descend on Ranger Judy's office. "We've got our first token," Derek says, pounding on the door. "We're ready for the next clue."

Brussels sprouts! We're already behind. I snatch the card out of Crispy's hand and read it out loud: "*What whole number yields the same result when added or multiplied?*"

"Two," Crispy says. "It's easy. Two plus two equals four. And two times two equals four. But what does it mean?"

"Two isn't a GPS coordinate and neither is four, at least not around here," Ronny says, tucking Xavier under her arm. "Unless it's twenty-four or forty-two. That might be part of a

GPS location." She taps her phone. "Right now, we're at lat 38 degrees and 42 minutes north, and long 78 degrees and 17 minutes west."

"So what's at two degrees latitude?" I ask out of curiosity. "And shouldn't there be minutes?"

"You don't need the minutes to know it's not around here." Ronny taps her phone again. "Lat two, long four is . . . in the Gulf of Guinea. Wherever that is."

"Not around here!" Crispy says. Freddie squeaks in agreement.

"The ranger said all the caches are within the campground," I say. "Let's look around for the number four."

"You mean the number *two*," Crispy corrects me.

"Let's go," I say, motioning Crispy and Ronny outside. Once outside, I glance around for anything obvious. Where would we find numbers in the campground? Four what? *Wait, Crispy is right.* The answer is two, not four. Two what?

"Two, two, two," I say under my breath. We race around the campground, trying to find something with the number two or a pair of something. A pair. A pair of what? I stop in my tracks. Each campsite is numbered. Ours is number ten. *What if . . .*

"Look!" Ronny is pointing at campsite number two.

We descend on the marker. A small box is attached to the pole with a plastic tie. I snap the box open. Sure enough, it contains four tokens: an eagle, a bear, a fox, and a deer. Was the Cheevers' first cache this easy? Must have been. That's how they found it so fast. The good news is if it was that easy for them, we'll find it fast too.

I pick the eagle token out of the box and snap it shut again. "Come on. Let's go get our second clue." My fist is closed so hard around the little plastic eagle that it's making dents in my palm. We've got to pick up our pace if we're going to beat Team Red Fox.

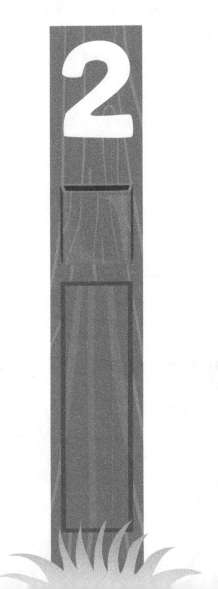

5

SAVE FREDDIE

THE THREE OF US DASH BACK to the Nature Center. I knock on Ranger Judy's office door. Breathless, I hand her the eagle token. "We're ready for the second clue."

"Does anyone need some water or a snack first?" she asks.

"Freddie is kind of hungry," Crispy says.

"You mean *you're* kind of hungry." I scowl at him. I dig into my spy vest and hand him some peanut butter crackers. "Here, eat this."

Crispy rips open the package, pops a cracker into his mouth, and then hands one to Freddie. The ferret sits up on Crispy's shoulder and holds the cracker in both paws, munching one end of it. They look like some sort of circus act.

I grab the cracker out of Freddie's paws. He squeaks and toots in protest. "No carbs for you." I reach into my spy vest again, pull out a piece of jerky, and hand it to the ferret. "Mom says you should eat meat."

Freddie gives me a dirty ferret look, but takes the jerky and gnaws on it.

"Just so you know," Ranger Judy says, "some clues are easy and some are more difficult."

"Yeah, that one was super easy," Crispy says with his mouth full.

I scowl at him again. I'm sure Ranger Judy doesn't want to see the contents of his mouth.

"Don't worry." She smiles. "I'm sure even you will find some of them pretty challenging."

I hold the door open, and Team Brown Bear files inside like I'm the doorman or something. They've already found their first token too. We're going to be in last place if we don't get a move on.

"Don't forget your GPS device." The ranger hands me another gold index card and winks.

"Thanks." I take the card.

"There are snacks and juice in the conference room." Ranger Judy leads us back there and points to a large table. Snacks are laid out along with bottles of water and orange juice.

"Cookies!" Ronny says, lunging for the plate of chocolate chip cookies.

Mom would have kittens if she knew how much gluten we were eating on this trip. I grab a cookie and pull up a chair.

"This one is longer," I say. "Listen. *With seconds to go, you'll find this cache just in the nick of time.*"

I glance at Crispy and Ronny, who are stuffing their faces with cookies. Then I continue, "*A fishmonger is 1.8576 meters tall, wears a size 33 jeans and an XXL shirt. What does he weigh?*" I look up. "That's it. That the clue."

"Read it again," Ronny says.

I read it again.

"What does he weigh?" I repeat. "There isn't enough information there to figure out what he weighs."

"It's a riddle," Crispy says. "You can't take it literally. In riddles, words can have double meanings."

"And in geocache puzzles, there can be all kinds of clues," Ronny says. "Even hidden in the instructions. They can be anywhere or anything."

"So being a geocacher is kind of like being a detective," I say. "Anything can be a possible clue."

Ronny nods and grabs another cookie. "Anything," she says as she takes a big bite. "Even random stuff."

"Guys, guys, guess what!" Gabby bursts into the room. "Ooh, cookies." She scoots into a chair next to Crispy and takes a cookie from the plate. "We found the first one." She puts her cookie on top of a napkin and then tickles Freddie's nose with the end of one of her braids. "I love him. He's so-o-o cute. Does he like cookies?" She holds her cookie out to Freddie, who grabs it and chomps it down.

"Who doesn't like cookies?" Ronny says.

I shake my head. "No more cookies for the ferret. He's supposed to be on a diet, remember?"

Gabby takes another cookie, puts it on a napkin, and hands it to her older brother. Marco nibbles it in silence. "We were running all over, and then Marco saw it." Gabby takes a bite of her cookie. "He's really good at puzzles and games. Have you guys ever played the game *Stare!?* Marco always wins." No wonder her name is Gabby—the girl can't stop talking.

"Hey, Gabby," I say. "Have you seen Kiki? We never got her back yesterday."

"You mean that cute little bear?" Gabby cracks open an orange juice. "The travel bug you're taking to the zoo?" She shakes her head. "I gave it to Marco, and he gave it to another kid. We just wanted to see it."

"Marco?" I turn to Gabby's brother. "Have you seen Kiki since you passed her around yesterday?"

Marco looks sullen. He stares down at his cookie.

"He hasn't seen the little bear either," Gabby says. She takes a swig of her juice.

I give her the side-eye. Why is she answering for her brother? Maybe Marco would talk more if he could get a word in edgewise.

Crispy picks up the index card off the table. "What's a fishmonger?"

"Someone who sells fish," I say.

"Fishmonger . . . 1.8576 meters tall . . . size 33 jeans . . . XXL shirt. What does he weigh?" Crispy squints at the card.

"Fish," Marco says.

I stare at him. *So he* can *talk*. "Fish?"

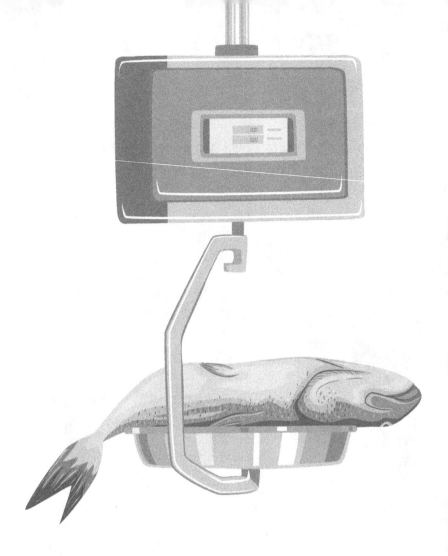

"He weighs fish," he says.

"A fishmonger weighs fish," Crispy says. "That's the answer."

"How does that help us find the next cache?" I ask. "Are there fish somewhere in the campground? Maybe a fishing hole? Maybe by the creek?"

"It's a red herring," Marco says.

"How do you know the fish is a herring?" Gabby asks. "Maybe it's a salmon."

"The clue doesn't say what kind of fish the monger sells." Ronny is done eating and back to dribbling her soccer ball. "So you can't know it's a herring."

"I think he means *red herring* as in a false clue." I scratch my head. "So what's the real clue?"

"What about the numbers?" Crispy asks. "The last answer was a number. And the ranger said we'd need the GPS."

"Seconds!" Ronny says. "The clue starts with *seconds to go*." She stops Xavier with her foot, then slips her phone out of her shorts pocket. "Let me see that card."

Crispy passes the card down the table to Ronny. Looking at the card, Ronny starts tapping her phone. "1.8576," she whispers. "Yup. It's seconds." She looks up from her phone.

"What do you mean, seconds?" I ask.

"Seconds on the GPS," Gabby says. "Don't you know how to use a GPS?"

"Not very well," I admit.

"Remember when I looked up our coordinates?" Ronny asks. "Our latitude is 38 degrees and 42 minutes north. Our longitude is 78 degrees and 17 minutes west."

"Yeah . . ."

"Well, that doesn't include the seconds."

I take off my glasses and rub my eyes. *Degrees. Minutes. Seconds.* I'm really confused.

"I get it," Crispy says. "It's that 1.8576 are the seconds in the GPS coordinates. What about the jeans, size 33? Is that seconds too?"

Ronny taps her phone. "When I add 1.8576 seconds to our lat and 33 seconds to our long, I get a location right here in the park near this campground." She's beaming. "It's really close!"

"Let's go," I say. "We've got to catch up to Over-a-Cheevers."

"The Cheevers are like professionals," Gabby says. "No one can catch them."

"You know them?" I ask.

"We do a lot of geocaching—"

"They're legendary," Marco interrupts.

"All the more reason to get going," I say. "Come on."

"Bye-bye," Gabby says as we take off after our next token. "Good luck, guys."

Even though it's not yet noon, the sun is heating up. It feels good after the air conditioning inside. The air smells like pinecones and burned-out campfires.

Ronny leads us to the coordinates. "Here," she says, glancing around.

We're standing at the trailhead that leads to Rose River Falls. Dad says this park is full of waterfalls. Yesterday, he took us to one, and it was great. We stood under the water like it was a shower.

"Are we supposed to take this trail?" Crispy asks.

"The ranger said all the caches were close to the campground." I scan the area for something out of the ordinary, something that shouldn't be there, like a box or bag or something.

There are trees as far as I can see, and the sounds of birds and chipmunks and other critters cheer us on. I take a deep breath. I like it out here. We have forests back home too. But not as wild as this.

"See anything?" I turn in a circle, carefully scoping out the area.

"Gabby seems nice," Ronny says. "But her brother is kind of weird."

Where did that come from? Talk about random comments.

"What's so weird about not wanting to talk all the time?" I ask. "Not everyone is a chatterbox like you."

"Look!" Crispy says.

I whip my head around. He's pointing at a tree. Freddie's standing on his shoulder, staring at a tree branch. "Did you find it?" I shield my eyes with my hand and focus on the tree. I don't see anything except branches, leaves, and a squirrel. The squirrel isn't happy we're invading his space. He's twitching his tail and scolding us.

Freddie chirps. Maybe they're having a conversation. Crispy claims our petting zoo animals talk to him. I should ask him if he understands squirrel.

"See it?" Crispy jabs his finger into the air. "There's a box in that tree."

I still don't see a box. "I see this red cord wrapped around the trunk." I move closer to the tree and touch the cord.

"Stand where I'm standing," Crispy says. "I think you can only see the box from this angle."

I move to where Crispy was standing. *Holy hideaway!* Now I see it: a bright orange box inside a hole in the tree trunk. "It's up pretty far." I go over to the tree trunk and reach for the box. *Brussels sprouts!* Too short. And if I can't reach it, Crispy and Ronny can forget it—they're pip-squeaks.

"Too bad we don't have a ladder," Ronny says, bouncing Xavier off her knee.

"I can climb up and get it," Crispy says.

"No way." I glare at him. "If you fall and get another concussion, Dad will have puppies. You don't want to go to the hospital again, do you?" It was only a couple of weeks ago that Crispy smacked his head on a branch while riding Spittoon. I found him unconscious under the tree . . . Believe me, it wasn't pretty, And I'm not letting it happen again.

I step back to gauge the distance from the ground up to the hole. "I have an idea. Ronny, do you think you can kick your soccer ball that high?"

"Of course." She drop-kicks Xavier and hits just above the hole. "See, easy peasy." She catches the ball when it bounces back.

"You missed," Crispy says.

"Do you think you can hit the box inside and knock it out?" I ask.

"I'll try." Ronny glances up at the hole, down to her foot, then back up to the hole. She bites her lip, narrows her eyes, and . . .

Smack. Dead center! She's a terror with that ball.

The soccer ball knocks the box deeper into the hole. *Slimy okra! Now how are we going to get it out?*

"Can you kick this into the hole?" Crispy asks, holding up a piece of kibble. Freddie gets excited, thinking it's for him. He snatches the kibble out of Crispy's fingers and wolfs it down.

"Are you kidding?" Ronny laughs. "Kick a tiny piece of dog food all the way up that tree? No way."

Crispy pulls another kibble from his pants pocket. He cocks his arm and launches the kibble toward the hole. Freddie launches himself off Crispy's shoulders and follows the kibble to the base of the tree, where it landed.

I shudder. The last time Freddie followed a dog biscuit into the forest, we didn't find him for days.

Crispy grabs at my spy vest, and I jump back. "Hey, what do you think you're doing?"

"Got any emergency dog biscuits?" he asks.

I fish one out and hand it to him.

Before his fingers even close, Freddie's back on his shoulder, reaching for the snack. Crispy winds up his arm like a baseball pitcher and lobs the biscuit at the tree.

Holy hot dog biscuit! He hits the bull's-eye: the biscuit lands right in the hole. And guess who follows it up?

"Freddie, bring the box down," Crispy says. "Get it, boy. Come on. Fetch."

I roll my eyes. Freddie scurries up the tree and disappears into the hole.

"Ferrets are pretty smart," Crispy says. "They can be taught to fetch."

I hope he taught Freddie to fetch.

"Get it, Freddie!" Ronny shouts. "You can do it!"

Freddie pokes his head out and looks down at us, holding the dog biscuit in both hands. He gnaws on it.

"Come on, Freddie," I join in. "Pretend it's a set of keys!" That's his favorite thing to steal.

Freddie finishes the biscuit and then washes his face with his paws.

"Come on, boy," Crispy says, patting his own shoulder. "Come back. Bring me the box."

Freddie ignores us. When he finishes his bath, he disappears back into the hole.

"I hope nobody lives in there," Crispy says. "Do you think he's okay?"

"I'm sure he's fine." I hope I'm right. An eagle or a hawk would love to snack on a ferret. I swallow hard and try not to think about birds of prey. "Freddie, come back. Come on, boy," I say in a singsong voice.

A scream comes from the hole. I glance over at Crispy. The color has drained from his face.

6

SABOTAGE

FREDDIE LEAPS OUT OF THE HOLE and scurries down the tree trunk. An angry blue jay swoops after him. The bird's squawking and Freddie's chirping and Crispy's freaking out. My heart is racing. *Is Freddie okay? Did that crazy bird peck his eye out or something?*

Freddie leaps off the tree trunk and lands on Crispy's shoulder. Crispy grabs the ferret with both hands. "Freddie! Are you okay, boy?" He cuddles Freddie and kisses him on the head.

That's when I see it. "Freddie, you did it!" I take the small box out of Freddie's mouth. He was holding it in his mouth by a cord wrapped around it, a red cord that matches the cord tied

to the tree trunk. "Freddie got the box." I pet the ferret's head. "Good boy, Freddie." He makes a little purring sound.

The box is just big enough for four tokens, but two are already gone. Team Red Fox and Team White-Tailed Deer have already been here. *Holy heights.* How'd Gabby and Marco manage to get all the way up that tree? The real hard part would be putting the box back up in the hole. *How are we going to do that?*

"Do you think we can get Freddie to put the box back?" I ask. "I mean, aren't we supposed to leave the cache exactly where we found it?"

"Freddie's not going back up there with that killer bird," Crispy says, clutching the ferret even tighter.

"Can you kick the box back up there?" I ask Ronny.

She shakes her head. "It's not heavy enough to kick that high. Why don't we just tie it onto that cord?"

"Then it will be so easy to find." I guess we don't really have a choice. Team Brown Bear is lucky we came before them. I retie the cord around the box, then tie it to the matching cord around the tree trunk.

"Wow, that one was tricky," Crispy says as we head back to the Nature Center. "I'm ready for lunch." Freddie squeaks in agreement. I guess the dog biscuit was only an appetizer.

"Me too," Ronny says.

"You guys are as bad as Freddie. All you want to do is eat." My stomach growls. I pick up my pace. Truth be told, I'm hungry too.

The sun is heating up, and I'm sweating like a pig— although technically pigs don't sweat. Even with all the trees and the shade, it's still hot. My cheeks are on fire. You don't even want to know what I look like when I'm overheated. I probably look like a tomato.

We pass the Cheevers on their way to their next cache. Either they already ate or they're skipping lunch.

As they walk by, Derek calls out, "Give it up, Golden Eagles. No way you'll catch up to us."

Kaboom echoes his older brother. "Yeah, give it up. We're winning."

They start chanting, "We're number one! We're number one!" Even Bethany joins in. They march through the campgrounds, chanting and pumping their fists in the air.

Grrr . . . I really, really, really hope we can beat them.

We're almost back to the Nature Center when Bobby Marino catches up to us.

"Hey, Red," he says. "What cache are you on? We're on our third."

Double grrr . . . I hate that nickname, and I hate losing. "My name is *Kassy*, and we're on our second, if you must know."

"Don't worry, *Kassy*." Bobby pokes me in the arm with his pudgy finger. "You'll catch up. It's just a dumb game." He takes off sprinting toward the Nature Center. A second later, the rest of Team Brown Bear zip past us.

Are we the slowest team in the contest? What gives?

Crispy and Ronny are kicking the soccer ball back and forth. *Don't they take this seriously?*

"Come on, slowpokes." I start jogging toward the entrance. "Hurry up!"

Inside, excited voices make for a lot of noise. Team Brown Bear and Team White-Tailed Deer are eating in the conference room. The park rangers have set up bagged lunches with sodas, chips, and everything. My stomach grumbles. I never get to have chips and soda at home. I can't wait to dig in.

I take three paper bags from the center of the table and hand one to each of my accomplices. They scoot into chairs on either side of our new friend Gabby, who's busy gabbing with Bobby from across the table. I grab three bags of chips and toss a couple of them over to Crispy and Ronny. Freddie is switching his tail around. Obviously, he's excited about lunch too.

"Want a soda?" I pick up a can for myself and set my spread on the table next to Crispy.

Of course they want sodas. I bring them their drinks and then settle in to see what's inside the bag. An apple, another cookie, and a sandwich—looks like peanut butter and jelly. I should have known. Freddie loves peanut butter.

Crispy pulls his sandwich out of its baggie, and Freddie immediately grabs it away from him. That ferret really needs to learn some manners . . . and also improve his diet.

"So, Ky, are you a boy or a girl?" Gabby asks. I just about choke on my sandwich. Gabby isn't shy, that's for sure.

"Depends," Ky says.

"On what?"

"On whether the problem at hand would be best solved by thinking like a girl or thinking like a boy." Ky takes a bite of apple.

Gabby thinks for a minute. "That makes sense."

Do I think like a girl? I mean, I'm a girl. But to be a good reporter, I need to put myself in other people's shoes, including boys'. It must be pretty handy to think like both.

Gabby turns to Ronny. "Hey, I saw you guys at the tree cache. What were you doing?"

"That was a hard one," Ronny says. "We almost didn't get it."

"But thanks to Freddie, we did," Crispy says. "Right, Freddie?" At the sound of his name, Freddie chirps.

"What?" Marco asks. "That one was a cinch." He must be good at climbing trees.

"Well, it was pretty far up there." I rub the apple on my shirt.

"No, it wasn't," Gabby says. "I could reach it, and I'm a lot shorter than you."

Crispy and I look at each other. *Chicken-fried steak.* The cord around the tree trunk—that's why it matched the cord around the cache box. It must have been tied to that cord before someone moved it . . .

Someone wants us to lose. And I have a pretty good idea who.

7

GOATS, DEVILS, AND UNICORNS

ONLY THE DEER AND FOX TOKENS were missing from that cache. Gabby and Marco didn't move the box, so that leaves the Cheevers.

Game on, Team Red Fox.

"Hurry up and eat," I say to my teammates. "We've got to catch up to the Cheevers."

"But I'm still hungry," Crispy whines.

"Yeah, because Freddie ate your sandwich, which isn't good for him. Remember what Mom said about ferret nutrition." I break off half of mine. "Here, have this."

"Okay, kids, listen up." Ranger Judy appears in the doorway. "When you finish eating, be sure to throw your garbage

68

away." She points to a giant trash bin next to the door. "And most importantly, have fun."

"We're ready for our next clue," I say, holding up our token.

"Good job," she says. "Come with me to my office."

I follow her out, wondering whether I should rat out the Cheevers. *Or maybe I should tell her someone took Kiki.*

"Did anyone turn in a koala bear charm?" I ask. Maybe Kiki ended up in the lost and found.

"A koala bear charm . . . I don't think so. But let me look."

I stand in the doorway to her office and watch her riffle through the bottom drawer of her desk.

"Nope. No koala bear was turned in." She glances up. "Sorry."

"Okay. Thanks." Did someone take Kiki on purpose—a.k.a. steal her—or is she just lost?

"But here's your next clue!" Ranger Judy hands me the gold index card. "Remember, some of them are pretty tricky. So take your time. And have fun!"

I glance at the card. The clue is just one riddle. I'll show it to Crispy, the riddle master. *Hopefully, those slowpokes are done eating.*

As I walk into the conference room, Bobby Marino throws a banana peel, and it hits me in the arm. I scowl. "What did you do that for?"

He shrugs and grins.

I shake my head. *Boys are the worst. Maybe thinking like a boy isn't always so great.*

I sit next to Crispy again. "What do you make of this?" I hand him the index card.

"Let me see it." Ronny scoots closer to Crispy and leans in.

Crispy reads it out loud. "*Good luck finding your next cache and be sure to stop and look for wildlife along the way!*"

"That's part of the clue," Ronny says.

Crispy glances over at me. "It's a what-am-I riddle. My favorite."

"Great, smarty-pants. Can you solve it?" I read the riddle in a low voice. "*I'm a king without a crown. What am I?*"

"A lion!" Gabby says.

"I knew that." Crispy glares at her.

"Where do we find a lion?" I wonder out loud.

"Up a tree," a voice says from behind me.

I swivel around and see Derek Cheever standing in the doorway, grinning. *What a jerk.*

"Come on," I say to Crispy and Ronny. "There's something rotten in here." I give Derek the side-eye.

After we toss our trash in the bin, we head out to the lobby. I circle the exhibits, wondering where we should go next. "A lion . . . Where do we find a lion?"

I mean, there could be *mountain* lions in Shenandoah National Park, but we can't find one. Mountain lions are notorious for being sneaky and hard to track. Anyway, we don't want to come face-to-face with a wild *Puma concolor,* otherwise known as a cougar.

Apollo, our baby cougar back at home in our petting zoo, was found abandoned, and he's used to us. But I wouldn't want to encounter a baby cougar in the wild. . . . Its mom might think I'm a tasty treat.

Crispy and Ronny follow me around the room. As if reading my mind, on the way out, Crispy pipes up, "*Puma concolor* have lots of different names. Mountain lion, puma, cougar. But they're all the same species."

"What are we doing?" Ronny asks, spinning her soccer ball on one finger.

"Thinking." *Could the riddle have a double meaning?* I make another lap around the exhibits and find myself face-to-face with the stuffed lynx. "Does a lynx count as a lion?" I lean in to examine the cat. Its beady eyes stare back at me. Stuffed animals give me the creeps. I mean, not stuffed toy animals but stuffed real animals.

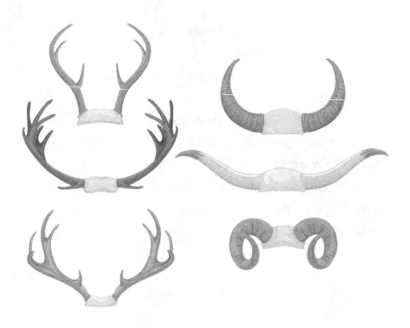

"Actually," Crispy says, "*Felis lynx* are a different species of cat than mountain lions."

"Whatever." Mangy maw! I see it. A slip of paper in its mouth. I snatch it out and read it out loud.

"*I'm shared by goats, devils, and unicorns. What am I?*"

Crispy repeats the riddle. I spin around the lobby, looking for goats, devils, or unicorns. Well, maybe just goats.

"Over here." Crispy dashes off to a corner with a big wall plaque describing the difference between antlers and . . . horns!

Deer and elk have antlers, which are shed and regrown every year. Sheep, goats, and bison have horns, which never shed. They continue to grow throughout the animal's life.

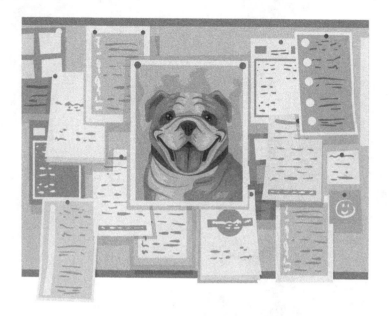

Another slip of paper is taped to a picture of a mountain goat. I peel it off and read it. *"I'm a dog that chases anything red. What am I?"*

"A red dog!" Ronny says.

I zip over to the fox exhibit. Maybe the clue means a red fox.

"The dog isn't red," Crispy says. "It *chases* something red."

"A red ball!" Ronny says.

"A dog isn't a wild animal." I scrunch my face to think. "There are dogs in the campground."

"Yara!" Ronny says.

"Does Yara chase anything red?"

"Yara chases her tail."

"Her tail isn't red." I start pacing around the lobby again. Walking helps me concentrate. On my next rotation around

the room, I notice a bulletin board with pictures of lost pets. "Wait a minute." I point to a picture of a bulldog with its tongue hanging out.

"Good one!" Crispy says.

"Huh?" Ronny doesn't get it.

"A bull chases anything red. Bull . . . dog." Crispy points at the picture. "See, bulldog."

We still haven't found the cache with the tokens. So there must be more clues. I search the bulletin board.

Crispy comes up behind me. "Got it." He pulls another slip of paper out from under the dog's picture. He reads it out loud. "*I'm an insect's favorite sport. What am I?*"

Freddie chirps.

"Do you know the answer?" my brother asks his ferret.

I roll my eyes and groan. Here we go again.

"What?" Crispy pouts. "Freddie likes insects. Especially crickets. He eats them like candy. And they're good for him."

"Crickets! Crispy, you're a genius." I scan the lobby for crickets. There must be one someplace. "Look for a cricket."

"Why a cricket?" Ronny asks.

"Or something that eats crickets," I say.

"An insect's favorite sport is cricket," Crispy says. "Who else in this room eats crickets?"

"Besides Freddie?"

"Snakes!" Crispy says. "Snakes eat crickets."

The snake exhibit has a stuffed snake in a glass aquarium. Its mouth is open wide next to a stuffed mouse. If the mouse is dinner, are crickets dessert?

I bend down and examine the aquarium, looking for another clue. Next to one corner of the glass box is a small blue bag closed with a drawstring. I pick it up and open it. *Aha!* The tokens are inside. We found the cache. I palm the eagle token and pull the drawstring shut. As I put the little bag back, something shiny on the floor catches my eye. I bend down and grab it.

"Look, it's Kiki's bracelet." I hold it up. *Who was standing near the snake exhibit when Kiki disappeared?* He, she, or they are our culprit.

8

RONNY'S SOCCER BALL

AT FIVE O'CLOCK, ALL THE TEAMS gather in the Nature Center lobby. Gabby is tickling a stuffed rabbit with the end of one of her pigtails. Derek Cheever and his siblings are high-fiving each other. Ky and their sisters are huddled in a corner, probably planning their strategy for tomorrow's hunt. Jimmy's pulling one of the girls' hair. And Bobby is . . . staring over at me. I look away.

"Kids, attention," Ranger Judy says. "Good job today, everyone. After your first day, Team Red Fox is in the lead, Team Golden Eagle is in second place, followed by team Brown Bear, and then team White-Tailed Deer. Go tell your folks how well you did, and rest up for tomorrow." She waves. "See you back here at nine sharp."

Another day closer to leaving without Kiki. *Brussels sprouts.* Ronny has crayons and paper back at our campsite. Maybe if we offer a reward, someone will return her.

I run up to Ranger Judy. "Excuse me," I say. "Would it be okay to post a flyer on your bulletin board about Kiki, our missing koala bear charm?"

"Sure. No problem."

"You're joking. A reward for a koala charm?" Dad shakes his head. "Just put up the sign. I'm sure if someone finds it, they'll return it."

Ronny fetches her crayons and some paper, and we sit around the picnic table. We can post one flyer on the bulletin board and a few others around the campground.

"I wish we had a reward," I whisper.

"I have this." Ronny holds up a brand-new *Dora la Exploradora* coloring book. "We could offer it as a reward."

"Wow. You'd give up your new coloring book?" Sometimes Ronny's not so bad.

Crispy pulls some small plastic figures from his pants pocket. "I have these plastic storm troopers . . . and a Yoda." His face falls. "Yoda's my favorite."

"Keep your Yoda." I pat my spy vest. What do I have to offer? A stale granola bar? My extra pencil? Most of my supplies are essential, so I can't give them away. "Let's try the coloring book and the storm troopers—if you're sure you're okay with that, Ronny."

She nods. "As long as we get Kiki back." She looks sad when she hands me the Dora coloring book. "The important thing is to get her to the zoo."

"Don't worry. We won't leave without her." I hope I'm right. If Dad gets the new tires on Monday, that leaves us one more day to find Kiki . . . and win the treasure hunt, of course.

We make two flyers each. I'm not sure a Dora coloring book and a couple of plastic storm troopers will be much of a lure for a hardened thief, but it's worth a try.

We hurry back to the Nature Center to post the flyer before Ranger Judy leaves for the night. We post one on the bulletin board, one on the outside door, and one on each bathroom door, and the other two on light posts in the campground.

On the way back to our campsite, the Cheevers appear on the path, blocking our way.

"How about a game of soccer?" Kaboom says. "We'll kick your butts."

"Let us pass," I say.

"Afraid you'll lose?" Derek asks.

"Leave them alone," Bethany says. "They're chickens. Not worth the trouble."

That really gets my goat—no offense, Han Solo. I'm not a soccer player, but boy, would I like to beat those Cheevers at *something*.

"We'll take you on," Ronny says. She bounces Xavier off her head, and Kaboom catches the ball.

I can't believe she's taking the bait. *Soggy collard greens.* I mean, Ronny is good, but there are three of them and just one Ronny!

I lag behind Crispy and Ronny as we follow the Cheevers to an open field near the campground.

"What can we use as goalposts?" Ronny asks. She actually seems excited about this challenge.

"I'll be right back," Kaboom says and then takes off running. A few minutes later, he returns with two sets of portable goalposts, nets and all.

My palms are sweating. I have a bad feeling about this.

"Flip for sides," Ronny says. "Anyone have a quarter?"

The Cheevers are ready with a quarter too. They came prepared.

I'm embarrassed to admit it, but I've never played soccer in my life. I've seen Crispy and Ronny kicking the ball around. But I have no idea of the rules or anything. I hang back and watch as the three Cheevers and Crispy and Ronny run around the field, kicking at the ball.

The first time Crispy kicks the ball, Freddie goes flying off his shoulder. The ferret comes scurrying over to me—poor guy must be desperate. I know how he feels.

"Kassy, get in here!" Ronny yells.

"What about Freddie?" Maybe I can use him as an excuse to stay on the sidelines.

"Fine, Percy and I will take them on." Ronny zips across the field like a lightning bolt.

"You and Freddie can guard the goal," Crispy says, chasing after the ball. "Just stand there and don't let the ball go into the net." He's jabbing his finger in the air, pointing toward one of the goals.

"Yeah, you be the goalie!" Ronny yells, still running like mad.

I lift Freddie onto my shoulders and take off for the goal-posts. *How hard can it be?* "We just stand here and keep the ball out of the net," I say to Freddie. *Geez.* I'm as bad as Crispy, talking to an animal.

Bethany is at the other goal, looking intense. Crispy, Ronny, Derek, and Kaboom are racing back and forth, kicking the ball up and down the field. I can barely see the ball. I have no idea how I'll be able to stop it.

Holy hurricane! Derek is running straight toward me. He kicks the ball. *Bam!* It hits me in the stomach, and I go flying into the net. My glasses—and Freddie—fly in the opposite direction. I'm gasping for breath, and my stomach hurts. "Did it go in?" I wheeze.

"Good save!" Ronny shouts.

"Does that mean I stopped the ball?"

"You did it." Crispy runs over and gives me a high five . . . well, a low five. I'm still lying on the ground. "Are you okay?"

"Yeah, I'm fine," I fib, staggering to my feet.

Freddie isn't so impressed. He climbs to the top of the net and looks down at me, flipping his tail around and scolding.

"Sorry about that," I say. But he just keeps chirping—and tooting—his disapproval.

I've barely brushed myself off before another ball is heading my way. I lunge at it . . . and do a face-plant in the grass. *Ouch!* This game hurts.

The Cheevers are hooting. I guess that means they scored. *Brussels sprouts.*

By the time I scrape myself off the ground again, Ronny is dribbling the ball down the field. She zips in between Derek and Kaboom and kicks the ball straight into the net. *Yes!*

Bethany throws the ball to Kaboom, and he starts coming my way. I grit my teeth and prepare for another hit. But just as he gets close, Ronny steals the ball away, zooms back across the field, and slices the ball into the corner of their net. *Wow. She's good.*

The game is going so fast, my head is spinning. Now Derek is coming at me with the ball. *Wait.* Now Crispy has it and is heading the other direction. He passes it to Ronny, she whizzes toward the goal—and Derek grabs her from behind, throwing her to the ground.

That's not fair. *Holy heartbreak.* She's hurt. She's holding her ankle and crying. I run to her as fast as I can.

"Are you okay?"

She shakes her head.

"Why did you do that?" I scream at Derek. "Look what you did to my sister, you bully!"

He shrugs. *What a jerk.*

"You're twice her size." I help Ronny stand up. She's limping pretty badly. I hope she's okay. "Let's go," I say to Crispy.

Freddie has already taken up his usual spot around my brother's neck. "We won anyway," Crispy says, joining Ronny and me.

"Oh yeah?" Kaboom says. He takes a running start and kicks the ball off into the woods.

"Xavier!" Ronny cries.

I sling an arm around her. "Don't worry. We'll find him."

Crispy and I help Ronny back to our campsite.

Mari rushes over to us. "What happened? Veronica, sweetie, are you okay?"

Ronny shakes her head, and more tears roll down her cheeks. "He grabbed me. So unfair."

"Who?" Mari asks, a concerned look on her face.

"That mean boy."

Mari dashes back to the RV. When she returns, she's carrying a case marked FIRST AID.

Crispy and I sit Ronny down at the picnic table.

"What about Xavier?" she asks through her tears. "How will I ever get him back?"

"We'll find him," I say. "I promise." *I have no idea how, but we will.*

While Mari wraps an elastic bandage around Ronny's ankle, I take out my notebook to make a list. So much has happened, and I have so many things to do. I need to write them down.

1. *Find Ronny's soccer ball in the woods.*

2. *Find Kiki. Most likely suspect—Derek "the Cheater" Cheever. Evidence: We found Kiki's bracelet near the snake exhibit, where the Cheevers were standing when she disappeared. More evidence: Derek is a jerk. I doubt he'll return Kiki for a coloring book or a few storm troopers.*

3. *Find out who slashed our tires. Most likely suspect— also Derek. Evidence: He has that big knife. More evidence: He's a jerk.*

4. *Win the geocaching treasure hunt and show those Cheevers who's boss. Why? See points 2 and 3 above.*

That night, when we're crammed into our little tent, I wait until I'm sure Dad and Mari are asleep. Then I wake up Crispy.

"What's going on?" he asks in a sleepy voice.

"Shhh." I put my finger to my lips. "Don't wake up Ronny. Come on." I struggle out of my sleeping bag. "We're going to find Xavier."

"Now?"

"Yup."

"It's dark out."

I dig my flashlight out of the pocket of my spy vest and click it on.

When Crispy sits up, Freddie yawns and climbs onto his shoulders.

I crawl out of the tent as quietly as I can so Ronny doesn't wake up. Crispy follows. Once we're outside, I slowly zip the tent back up.

I wore my clothes to bed, but Crispy's in his pajamas.

Oh well. No one is going to see us anyway.

Luckily, there's a full moon, so it's not as dark as it could be. Crispy and I head for the soccer field. It's going to be tricky to find a ball in the forest . . . in the dark . . . but for Ronny's sake, we've got to try.

The sounds in the forest at night are different from the sounds during the day. Instead of birds singing and chipmunks chirping, there are hoots and howls and insects buzzing. And bats! *Chicken-fried steak.* Now I'm convinced that every branch or leaf that touches my hair is a rabid bat.

Crispy and I start out on a trail. As we walk, I shine my light in all directions, looking for the soccer ball. It has reflective strips on it, so it should be easy to see if my light hits it. But what if we can't see it from the trail? We'll have to bushwhack.

"My feet hurt," Crispy whines. He's wearing his slippers, and there are rocks and roots on the trail. "I want to go back."

"Let's just look a little longer, okay?" Maybe I should have come out by myself. But I was scared. "Just five more minutes." If Dad finds out, we'll both be grounded.

"Okay."

Freddie squeaks, then leaps off Crispy's shoulders and dis-appears into the forest. Before I know it, Crispy is beating the bushes, running after him. So much for sore feet.

I chase after them, following the rustling sound of twigs and branches breaking. Some are whacking me in the face. I

have to hold my glasses in place with one hand and hold my flashlight with the other. Its beam is bouncing all over the place, and my heart is racing faster than my feet.

After a few minutes, the rustling sound stops, and so do I. *Brussels sprouts.* I have no idea where we are. A GPS device would come in handy about now.

I shine my light in all directions. Where are they? I listen in the darkness. Nothing. *Wait.* I hear chirping—Freddie! I take off in the direction of the noise.

Slamming through the underbrush like a moose, I break out into a small open patch. Freddie is sitting on top of the soccer ball, and Crispy is feeding him kibble. I shake my head. Yeah, my goofy brother even keeps dog food in his pajama pockets in case Freddie wants a midnight snack.

9

THE MISSING TOKEN

THE NEXT MORNING AT BREAKFAST, when Dad asks me where I got the scratches on my face, I blame Freddie.

"Freddie doesn't scratch!" Crispy says. The ferret joins the protest . . . you can guess how.

Dad just shakes his head. "You and that rodent of yours."

"Freddie is not a rodent," Crispy says. "He's *Mustela*—"

"I know, I know," Dad interrupts. "*Mustela putorius furo*, part of the weasel family."

Ronny is ecstatic to have Xavier back. But I swear her to secrecy about how we found him. Her ankle still hurts, but she's all smiles as she eats her cereal. She taps her phone. "We'd better hurry if we're going to get to the Nature Center by nine."

We finish our breakfast, help clear the table, and then head out.

"Be careful," Dad says.

"No more running," Mari says.

I nod. "Don't worry, we will . . . I mean, won't."

Once we're out of sight, we take off running toward the Nature Center. Ronny is still the fastest, even with a hurt ankle. She beats Crispy and me to the entrance.

All the teams—except the Brown Bears—are milling around the lobby, waiting for the next clues.

Gabby comes up to me. "Hey, what happened to your face?"

I glare at Derek the cheater. "Nothing. I'm fine."

Gabby points to Ronny's leg. "And your foot! Why do you have that bandage?"

"Soccer," Ronny says, hugging Xavier to her chest.

"But we won," Crispy adds.

"Not true," says Kaboom. "Game called because of a crybaby."

Grrr. I'd like to punch him. But I already look like I got beat up.

The office door swings open. "Settle down, kids!" Ranger Judy shouts on her way out to the lobby. "Today, one team will take home the grand prize. Ready for some fun?"

"Yes!" we all shout.

"I can't hear you . . ." She cups her hand around her ear.

Oh no. Not this again.

"*Yes!*" we shout back.

Ranger Judy passes index cards to the team captains. "Where are the Brown Bears?" she asks. "Has anyone seen the Marinos? Or Ky and their sisters?"

Everyone shakes their heads.

"They're late," the ranger says. "Oh well. It's all about having fun. Right, kids?"

She gets a couple of mumbles in response.

"I can't hear you!" She puts her hand to her ear again.

"*Right!*" we all shout at the top of our lungs.

Crispy, Ronny, and I huddle in one corner of the lobby with our card. I read the clue in a whisper: "*This old one runs forever but never moves at all. It has not lungs nor throat but still a mighty roaring call.*"

"That's it?" Ronny asks. "That's all it says?"

"Yup."

"Runs forever, never moves," Crispy repeats. "No lungs . . . but a mighty roar." He scratches his head, and Freddie licks his hand.

"Good luck, guys," Gabby says on her way out the door. Marco follows her with a sullen look on his face.

"Yeah, good luck, crybabies," Kaboom says in a mocking voice as he walks by.

I shoot him a dirty look.

When the Cheevers are gone, Ronny says, "What a bunch of cheaters. And they're not as good at soccer as they think they are."

"You ran circles around them," I say. It's true. I bet she'll play in the Olympics or something when she grows up. That's her dream, anyway.

Ky comes through the door followed by Bobby and Jimmy.

"Hey, Ky, you're late," I say.

"Yeah. Kaleigh and Kristy wouldn't budge. They've had enough geocaching. They just want to put on makeup and play games on their phones."

"Must be nice . . . not the makeup, the phone." My birthday is on Monday, and I've dropped enough hints to fill a swimming pool. I hope Mom and Dad have been listening.

"I guess so," Ky says. "Seems like a waste to be in a nice park like this and spend all day on your phone."

Now they're sounding like Mom. "You say that because *you* have a phone . . ."

"Ky, you'd better go get your clue," Ronny says. "The Cheevers already have a head start."

"Yeah, I'm surprised they're not back with their token by now," Crispy says. He hands Freddie a piece of kibble.

"I'd rather have a ferret than a phone," Ky says, petting Freddie on the head.

"Me too." Crispy smiles. "He's my best friend."

My little brother—his best friend is a ferret. And my step-sister—her best friend is a soccer ball. I shake my head. At least they have a best friend. I guess my best friend is Butler. But he had to stay home and help his mom with the bakery, where my detective office is in the back broom closet.

"A waterfall!" Crispy says.

"What?"

"The answer to the riddle." He's beaming. "It's a roaring waterfall."

I reread the card. "That makes sense. A waterfall runs for-ever but never moves. It doesn't have lungs or a throat, but it still has a mighty roaring call. Crispy, you're a genius." He may be a few sandwiches short of a picnic, but he sure is good at riddles.

"But what waterfall?" he asks.

"Are there any other clues on the card?" Ronny asks. "Any instructions or symbols or anything? Remember, anything can be a clue when it comes to geocaching."

I turn the card over in my hand. "Hey, it says *The Whiteoak Eagles* on the back."

"Did the other cards say *The Eagles* on them?" Crispy asks. "And why the Whiteoak Eagles? I thought we were the Golden Eagles."

"That must be another clue," Ronny says. "Is there a waterfall called Whiteoak around here?"

"Let's find out." I head over to the map posted on the wall. Crispy, Freddie, Ronny, and Xavier trail behind me. "Look." I point at a spot near the campground. "That must be it."

"Whiteoak Falls," Ronny says, reading off the map. "Let's go."

"The Cheevers aren't back yet." Crispy looks over his shoulder (and Freddie's head). "If we hurry, maybe we can get back before them and move into first place."

"Let's do it," I say, jogging toward the door.

The smell of pine trees and sunshine fills the air. It's warm but not hot yet . . . pretty much perfect. We're zipping to the trailhead when I spot the Cheevers coming out of the woods. *Slimy okra!* Did they find their cache already? We'll never catch up. I pick up my pace.

The trail is flat and wide and has nice shady trees on both sides. Within a couple of minutes, we're at the waterfall. Now where is the cache hidden? It's a small waterfall but a big area. It could be anywhere.

A wooden sign describes the geology of the rocks and the source of the water. I read the sign to see if it holds any clues.

"Look," Ronny says, pointing at a small box attached to the pole holding up the sign.

"There it is!" Crispy says. "Hurry! Maybe there's still time to beat the Cheevers."

I bend down, grab the box, and open it. *Wait. What?*

The eagle token is missing.

10
KIKI RETURNS

WE TRUDGE BACK TO THE NATURE CENTER. How can we win the contest if our tokens are gone?

I knock on the office door, and Ranger Judy answers. She's munching on a granola bar. "Hey, Golden Eagles. That was quick. Good job."

"We found the cache," I say. "But our token wasn't there."

"Hmm. That's odd." She frowns and wipes crumbs off her shirtfront. "Why don't you take your next clue? I'll look into the missing token." She gives me a questioning look. *Doesn't she believe me?* Does she think we didn't find the cache and so I'm making up a story?

Ronny holds up her phone. "See. The waterfall. We found it."

The ranger picks up another gold index card from her desk and then hands it to me. "You kids want a snack before you head out again?"

"We're good," I say. Actually, I'm starving. But we don't have time for snacks. We've got to get to the next cache and catch up to the cheating Cheevers.

Then again, this clue looks tough—it's split into three parts. "Come on." I lead Ronny and Crispy to the break room. I think we're going to need to sit down to figure this one out.

We sit at the end of the long table. Gabby and Marco are at the other end, helping themselves to juice and cookies. "Did you find the cache already?" Gabby asks.

"You guys didn't take our token by mistake, did you?" Crispy asks.

"What do you mean?" Gabby puts her cookie down.

"The eagle token was missing from our last cache," I say.

"Weird," Gabby says. "So was ours."

"Aren't you in a hurry to find the next one?" Ronny asks.

"We're going to lose anyway," Marco says. "We always lose."

"What do you mean?" I ask.

He just shrugs.

Ronny helps herself to a cookie and some orange juice. Crispy follows her lead. Freddie jumps off my brother's shoulders and helps himself too. Good thing Ranger Judy's not here to see that.

I snag the cookie out of Freddie's paws.

He toots in my face.

"Sorry, cookies aren't good for you, buddy."

I leave Freddie fuming, and I study the clues.

1. *Some live in me, and some live on me.*
Some cut me to walk upon.
I rarely leave my native land.
Until my death, I always stand.
High and low I may be found.
Both above and below the ground.
My rings may not mean we're engaged.
But they do tell you how much I've aged.

2. *I travel from coast to coast without moving.*

3. *I fly all day but never go anywhere.*

"What do you think?" I ask Crispy once he's settled back into his chair. I slide the card over to him.

He stares down at it while he munches his cookie. "I think the first one is a tree." He looks up at me.

"Since we're surrounded by trees, that's not very helpful." I grab a cookie. Maybe some sugar will help me concentrate.

"We need to solve the other two riddles," Ronny says. "Then maybe we'll know what tree." Xavier is sitting on her lap. Since his adventure in the woods, she hasn't let him out of her sight.

Ky, Jimmy, and Bobby burst into the break room.

"Did one of you take our token?" Jimmy asks.

We all shake our heads.

"Ours were taken too," Gabby says.

"Someone isn't playing by the rules," Ky says, grabbing a cookie and plopping down into a chair.

"The cheating Cheevers," I say under my breath.

"Someone is a thief." Ky glares over at their cousin Bobby. "*Someone* needs to return *stolen property*."

Bobby blushes and squirms in his chair. "Kassy, can I talk to you for a minute?" he asks.

What could Bobby want with me? I nod. "Okay, shoot."

"In private," he says, pointing to the door.

Okay. Now this is weird.

I follow him out the door and into the lobby.

He stops next to the snake exhibit. He's rocking from foot to foot like maybe he has to pee or something. Staring at the floor, he reaches into his pants pocket. "Here."

Holy hoodwink! It's Kiki the travel bug! "Where'd you find her?" I ask.

"I took her." He doesn't look up. "Sorry." His cheeks are red, and he looks like he might barf.

"Why?" I'm surprised Bobby wants a Dora coloring book and a few storm troopers. Maybe he's really into coloring. "Are you returning her now for the reward?"

"I don't want the reward." He glances up and gives me a weak smile.

"Why'd you take her?"

"I knew you wouldn't leave without her."

What?

"Why didn't you want us to leave?" *Holy hoodlum! Did Bobby slash our tires too so we couldn't leave?*

He shrugs. "I don't know." Now his face is the color of a tomato. "I'm really sorry . . . I shouldn't have done what I did."

I'm afraid to ask what else he did. I have a hunch he's the tire slasher. But since he returned Kiki, I don't really want to get him in trouble.

"Well, thanks for giving her back." I tuck the koala bear charm into my securest spy vest pocket and Velcro it shut for safekeeping.

"Good luck with the contest," Bobby says. "I hope you win."

"Thanks." I hope we win too.

Bobby and I go back into the break room.

Jimmy says, "Did you give your girlfriend back her stupid bear?"

"She's not my girlfriend," Bobby says.

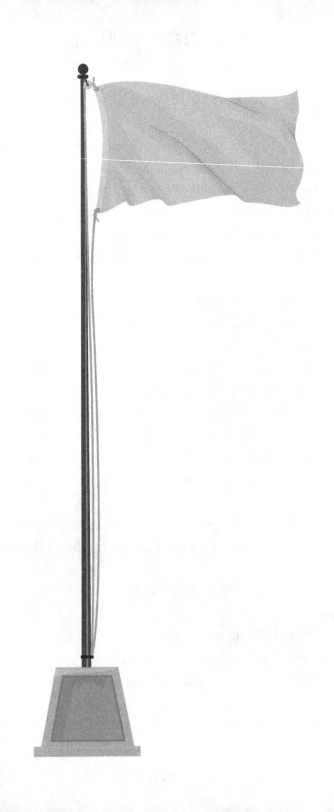

My cheeks are hot. Now *I* probably look like a tomato.

"Highway!" Crispy blurts out. "What travels from coast to coast but doesn't move? The answer to the riddle is a highway."

I zip to the end of the table and rejoin Crispy and Ronny. "So we're looking for a tree by the highway. That's a start. But there are still a lot of trees to choose from."

"Right," Crispy says.

"If we solve the last riddle, maybe we'll know what tree," Ronny says.

"Let's go." I can't wait to get out of the room and away from Jimmy and Bobby Marino. *If Bobby didn't want us to go, is he the tire slasher? So it wasn't Derek Cheever?* I'm confused.

As we cross the campground toward the highway, I see Dad and Mari arguing. I smile to myself. *Could that mean they're breaking up?* I like Mari, but she's not Mom. I wish Mom and Dad would get back together. Mom says there's no way. But I can always hope, can't I?

The dew on the grass is getting the toes of my hiking boots wet. The morning air is still cool and fresh, and I'm glad I wore a long-sleeved shirt.

Okay. So we're near the entrance to the park, just off the highway. And there are lots of trees. *Which one is it?*

I take the index card from my vest pocket and reread the last riddle. "What flies all day but never goes anywhere?" I glance around to see if anything looks like something that flies but goes nowhere. "What flies all day?"

"Birds," Ronny says.

"Bats," Crispy says. "Except they fly at night."

"Thank goodness." I shudder.

I start listing everything I can think of that flies: "Airplanes, kites, bees, flies, balloons . . ."

"Flags!" Crispy points at a flagpole. Freddie stands at attention on my brother's shoulders and looks up at the flag. You'd think the ferret was about to say the Pledge of Allegiance.

We all run to the flagpole. Nothing. No cache. Then I remember the first clue—I whip around, looking for any obvious tree nearby. The flagpole is in a small clearing at the park entrance. Next to it is a small flowering tree.

"Here." I crawl around under the tree, checking its trunk. Sure enough, there's a small box tied to a cord around its trunk. "I found it!"

I untie the cord and open the box. *Yes!* All the tokens are still here. I have an idea . . . a devious idea. "What if we take our token *and* the Cheevers' fox token, then trade with them to get our other eagle token back?"

"Good idea," Crispy says.

"What about the rules?" Ronny asks.

"They'll give us ours, and we'll give them theirs. In a way, we're helping them."

Ronny wrinkles her nose. "I guess that makes sense."

I pocket both tokens, then fasten the box back on the cord and retie it around the tree. Now to find the Cheevers and negotiate a trade. I'm not looking forward to facing off with Derek.

Speak of the deviled eggs. We're halfway back to the Nature Center when I see them. Team Red Fox is headed our way.

"Well, if it isn't Team Crybaby," Kaboom says with a chuckle.

Ha-ha. Very funny.

"Looking for this?" I hold up the fox token.

"Hey, where'd you get that?" Derek asks.

"From the last cache." I wave it in the air. "We'll trade you for our last eagle token."

Derek looks at Kaboom, and they both look at Bethany.

Is she the brains behind Team Red Fox?

"Hand it over," Derek says, his hand outstretched.

"Not until we get our eagle token." I plant my feet firmly in place and put my hands on my hips.

"How do we know we can trust you?" Bethany asks. "You go first."

How can they know they can trust us? *They're the untrustworthy ones.* "Come and get it," I say, holding it out on the palm of my hand.

"Kassy, what are you doing?" Crispy asks. "What if they take it *and* keep ours?"

"Then they'll have to admit they can't beat 'Team Crybaby' without cheating." I wiggle my fingers, beckoning Derek to take the token. "If they don't give us our token, that just proves they can't win fair and square."

Derek looks back at Kaboom and Bethany. His sister nods. He pulls the eagle token out of his pocket and snatches the fox token out of my hand. "We'll beat you no matter what," he says, then drops our token at my feet. "Go ahead. Pick it up, crybabies."

"At least we're not cheaters," I say, bending down to pick up our token. "Only one more cache to go. Whoever gets there first will be the winner." I blow the dirt off the token and put it in my pocket. "May the best team win."

11
WHAT AM I?

I DON'T TELL RANGER JUDY ABOUT the Cheevers taking our token. I want to win outright, not by disqualifying them.

The Cheevers are right behind us at the door to the ranger's office. But we get our clue first, so we have a few seconds' advantage.

I glance down at the index card. *Brussels sprouts!* Not that our head start will do us much good. The last clue is a doozy. It's going to be like decoding something from *Scooby Doo*. What does it even mean?

I hand the card to Crispy. "Wow," he says. "I need a cookie."

We head into the break room. Sitting at the table, I take out my notebook and pencil. We're going to need it to figure out this monster riddle.

Crispy and Ronny fill up paper plates with cheese cubes, crackers, apple slices, and, of course, cookies.

"Want some?" Ronny offers her plate to me.

I pick up a cube of cheese. "Thanks."

"That's a lot of riddles," Crispy says, squinting at the index card. Freddie chirps in agreement. "Let's figure them out one at a time."

"Good plan." I read out the first riddle. "*What is at the end of a rainbow?*"

"A pot of gold!" Ronny says.

"Is there any gold in this park?" I ask. "Maybe a gold mine or something?"

Ronny takes the index card out of Crispy's hand. "Wait. You didn't read the instructions." She holds the card up and reads: "*Mind your p's and q's. Dot your i's, and cross your t's.*"

"Letters?" I ask.

"Let's move on to the second riddle," Crispy says. "I have a hunch."

"Okay." I grab the card back and read the next riddle. "*It's in the church but not in the steeple. It's in the parson but not in the people. It's in the oyster but not in the shell. It's in the clapper but not in the bell.*"

"I think this is an alphabet riddle," Crispy says. "Concentrate on the letters."

"What do you mean?" I ask.

"What letters are in *church* but not in *steeple*, in *parson* but not in *people*, in *oyster* but not in *shell*, in *clapper* but not in *bell*?" Crispy scrapes the peanut butter off a cracker and feeds it to Freddie. At least he doesn't give him another cracker.

"*E!*" Ronny says.

"Parson doesn't have an *E*," I say.

"Oh yeah. Right." She takes a swig of juice.

"So what letter is in all these words: church, parson, oyster, and clapper?"

"*R*," Crispy says.

"Right. *R*." I write down *R* in my notebook.

"That makes me think our first answer's wrong." Crispy takes a bite of cookie. "It's not *pot of gold*. It's *W*."

Aha! I write a *W* in front of the *R* in my notebook. "Because the last letter in *rainbow* is *W*."

"Bingo. What's the next riddle?" Crispy asks.

"*I am the beginning of the end, and the end of time and space,*" I read off the card. "*I am essential to creation, and I surround every place. What am I?*"

"Is this another letter riddle?" Ronny asks.

"Yup," Crispy says. "Once you know it's a letter, it's easy."

"The beginning of the *end* and the end of *space . . . E,*" I say.

"Right." Crispy holds up his hand to high-five me, and Freddie licks his fingers. I high-five Crispy anyway, even though he has ferret juice on his hand.

"*W-R-E,*" I say, and then write *E* in my notebook. "Here's the next riddle: *What happens every second, minute, month, and century, but not every hour, week, year, or decade?*"

"So we're looking for a letter in *second, minute, month,* and *century* that isn't in *hour, week, year,* or *decade,* right?" Ronny asks.

"You're catching on," Crispy says.

"*T!*" Ronny says.

"There's no *T* in *second,*" I say. "What about *N*?" I write N in my notebook. "*W-R-E-N.* Wren."

"A wren is a type of bird," Crispy says. "Maybe we're looking for a wren."

"How could we find one particular wren in this whole campground?" I go back to the index card. We're only about halfway through the clues. Hopefully when we get all the way through them, it will all make sense.

I read the next riddle. "*I am the beginning of sorrow and the end of sickness. You cannot express happiness without me, yet I am in the midst of crosses. I am always in risk yet never in danger. You may find me in the sun, but I am never seen out of darkness.*"

"*S!*" Ronny shouts.

"You got it," Crispy says. He gives Ronny a sticky high five.

We're cruising right along. I glance across the table and see the Cheevers struggling with their clues too. We have to hurry. I read the next riddle. "*There is one in every corner and two in every room.*"

"*O,*" Crispy says. "Too easy."

I write *O* in my notebook. "*S-O.*"

"Read the next one."

"*I can be found in seconds, minutes, and centuries, but not in days, years, or decades.*" Didn't we already do that one? "Another *N*?"

"Yup," Crispy says. "Must be."

"*S-O-N* . . . *wren son.* Does that make sense?"

"The son of a bird?" Ronny asks.

"What's the next one?"

"Easy peasy," I say. "*What is the end of everything? G.*" I write a *G* in my notebook. "*S-O-N-G.*"

"Wren song," Crispy says. "Is there something called *wren song* in the park? Or maybe a place where a lot of wrens are singing?"

"I don't know, but there are more riddles on the back of the card." I turn it over.

"More riddles!" Ronny puts her head in her hands.

"Only two," I say. *Whew.* This is intense. I need a cookie. I snatch one off Ronny's plate and take a bite. "Here's the next one: *When I'm metal or wood, I help you get home. When I'm flesh and I'm blood, in the darkness I roam. What am I?*"

"It's a what-am-I riddle," Crispy says.

"Not another alphabet riddle?" I ask. "What am I?"

"That's a hard one," Ronny says. "Let's skip it and hear the last one."

"Okay." I hold up the card. "Here's the very last riddle. *On my own, I am darkness, a black abyss. I am quiet and cold, but warmth I can hold. My mouth is so large I swallow you whole. To be in my belly is your goal. For some, I am fear. For others, hope. From the earth I have come and forever will stay, even if parts of me crumble away. What am I?*"

"Another what-am-I riddle," Crispy says.

"I give up," Ronny says. "It's too hard."

"We can't give up," I say. "We've got to beat those cheating Cheevers." She's right, though. These last riddles are really hard. Even Crispy looks stumped.

The Cheevers are whispering and laughing. I can't take it anymore. "Let's get out of here." I pop the rest of my cookie into my mouth. "Maybe we'll see something outside that helps us solve those last two riddles."

"But which direction should we go?" Crispy asks. "All we know is *wren song.*"

"I have an idea." I throw Ronny's empty plate into the trash. "Come on." I head out to the lobby and over to the map on the wall. "Wren song," I whisper, running my finger over the map. "Wren song, wren song, wren song. . . . Aha!" I stab the map with my finger. "There. Wren Song Cave."

"It's just past our campsite," Crispy says.

Soggy collards! A cave. I get a fluttery feeling in the pit of my stomach like a wren is nesting in there. "*When I'm metal or wood, I help you get home. When I'm flesh and I'm blood, in the darkness I roam.*" My palms break out in a sweat. "I think I know the answer to the other riddle."

"What is it?" Ronny says. "Bears?"

"Cougars," Crispy says.

"No. Bats." *Just my luck: the last cache is hidden in a stinky bat cave.* I shudder just thinking about those gross flying rats nesting in my hair.

"Bats are cute," Gabby says, sneaking up behind me. "Are you guys going to Wren Song Bat Cave?"

I nod. "Unfortunately."

"That's where we're going too." She holds up their white card. "We can all go together."

I scrunch up my eyes. "So the last clue is the same for everybody?" That means the Cheevers will be going to the bat cave too. "Come on. We've got to hurry." I dash outside. The rest of Team Golden Eagle and Team White-Tailed Deer follow me.

We run as fast as we can across the campground. "Hurry!" I shout. "We've got to get there before the Cheevers."

"But the Red Foxes aren't in the—" Poor Gabby is struggling to keep up. I glance behind me. She's panting, and her face is all red. "Guys, wait up!"

I'm tempted to slow down, but then I hear the Cheevers whooping from across the campground. They've figured out the clues, and they're on their way to the cave. I pick up my pace. "Run!" I yell. "Hurry up!"

Ronny is out front, kicking Xavier as she goes. "Where's the cave?" she yells back to me.

"That direction." I point off to my left. "You're going the wrong way."

She stops the ball with her foot and takes off in the direction I'm pointing.

My lungs hurt from running so fast. But I can't stop now. We're ahead. We're going to beat the Cheevers. My heart is racing. I tell my legs to keep going. *Run, run faster.*

"There it is!" I see the cave up ahead. Ronny is standing at the entrance, spinning Xavier on her finger . . . when she *should* be finding the cache.

Holy yuck. Three bats fly over Ronny's head. I get a lump in my throat and feel like turning back. *You mean I have to go inside that cave with those bats? Yes, Kassy, you do.* "You can do it," I tell myself. "They're harmless insect-eaters."

At the mouth of the cave, I swallow hard and take a deep breath. *Here goes.* A bat swoops at my head, and I scream.

I hear someone else screaming too. I stop and listen. *Wait. That's Gabby.* She's screaming for help. My chest tightens. I glance inside the cave and see a flashing light. That must be the cache.

Gabby is crying now and screaming like she's in pain. *Chicken-fried steak!*

Ronny takes off back down the path toward the screams. Crispy follows her.

What should I do? I bite my lip until it hurts. Go after the cache to win the treasure hunt? Or go help poor Gabby?

Her cries are getting worse. I'm scared. I take off running as fast as I can back down the path.

12

AND THE WINNER IS...

GABBY IS SITTING ON THE GROUND, crying. Her shirt is covered in grass stains, and her face is all dirty. One of her pigtails has come loose.

Marco's standing over her. He looks worried. "She was running and twisted her ankle in a gopher hole," he says. "Hopefully, it's not broken."

I pull the GPS device from my back pocket and depress the walkie-talkie button. "Ranger Judy, please come in." Nothing but static. "It's an emergency." More static.

"Let's carry her," Marco says.

Marco and I basically have to carry her back to the Nature Center. She can't put any weight on her ankle without howling in pain.

"It hurts," she says over and over again.

We're almost to the door of the Nature Center when the Cheevers run past us, hooting and jeering.

"We won! So there, crybabies!" Kaboom yells as he runs by.

What a jerk. Of course he doesn't care Gabby's hurt. I feel my face turning red. I'm fighting back tears. You'd think *I* was the one with the twisted ankle.

"Ignore them," Marco says. "They're not worth the trouble."

He's right.

By the time we limp into the Nature Center, Team Red Fox and Team Brown Bear are already sitting around the conference table, enjoying cool lemonade and gingersnaps. The Cheevers are sitting at one end of the table, gloating. They're all smiles, so happy they've won. Ky and their cousins are at the other end. Jimmy and Bobby are poking each other and growling. They really do look like bears.

"Knock it off," Ky says, flipping their hair over their shoulder. "You two are so immature." The Marino brothers keep right on prodding each other. Ky jumps up when we carry Gabby into the room. "What happened?"

"She hurt her ankle." I point to her foot. "She can't walk."

Poor Gabby is sniffling but putting on a brave face now in front of the others.

"What's going on?" Ranger Judy appears in the doorway, an anxious look on her face. "What happened?"

Sucking in her breath, Gabby tells the ranger about her accident.

"Put your foot up." The ranger scoots a chair closer to where Gabby is sitting, and Gabby puts her foot up on it. "I'll go get some ice."

A few seconds later, she reappears with an ice pack. "This will be cold, but it will help a lot." She carefully lays the ice pack across Gabby's ankle. "Kassy, why don't you get Gabby some lemonade while I get the first aid kit?"

I bring Gabby a glass of lemonade, and she gives me a weak smile. "It will be okay," I say. I hope I'm right.

Gabby's face is as white as the index card clutched in her little hand. She's probably in shock. *I wish Mom were here. She always knows what to do.* She may be a veterinarian, but she's pretty good at doctoring people too.

"You'll have a bandage around your ankle just like me," Ronny says. "Then we'll be twins."

Gabby smiles through her tears.

When the ranger returns with the first aid kit, the Cheevers start grousing.

"Hey, how about you announce the winners?" Derek says.

"We want our prize," Kaboom says.

Ranger Judy tightens her lips but doesn't say anything. She wipes Gabby's face with a damp cloth. "I've called for a doctor. You'll be okay." She pushes a loose strand of hair back behind Gabby's ear. "I guess that's all we can do for now. Maybe a cookie will make you feel better?"

Gabby nods.

I fetch her a plate piled high with gingersnaps and set it in front of her.

"When are you going to give out the prizes?" Derek asks.

"Settle down," Ranger Judy says. She adjusts the ice pack, then riffles through the first aid kit. "We'll probably wrap it. But first let's have the doctor take a look."

"Since we have to wait, we might as well get the prizes," Bethany says, kicking her boots up on the table.

"Please take your feet off the table."

Bethany makes as much noise as she can putting her feet down.

"Okay, kids," Ranger Judy says. "We might as well announce the winners and give out the prizes while we wait." She disappears

again and comes back with the tent in her hands and a box tucked under one arm. She drops the tent on the table. Then she opens the box, pulls out a white ribbon, and waves it in the air.

"Fourth place." She holds up a deer charm. "Goes to Team White-Tailed Deer. Congratulations." She hands the ribbon and the charm to Gabby.

"Last place, more like," Kaboom says. His siblings laugh.

I just shake my head.

She pulls out a red ribbon. "In third place . . ." She takes an eagle charm out of the box. "We have Team Golden Eagle." She hands the ribbon and eagle charm to me.

Sigh. I guess I'll be sleeping in that tent with Crispy, Freddie, Ronny, Xavier, Yara, and Han Solo. *Oh well.* I won't get lonely, that's for sure.

"They're the Crybabies, not the Eagles."

Jerk.

"Settle down, please," Ranger Judy says. She takes a red ribbon from the box. "And in second place, we have Team Red Fox." She hands the ribbon and a fox charm to Derek.

Wait—what? The Cheevers didn't win? I'm almost as happy as if we did win.

"No way," Derek says, tossing the charm across the table. "We won. We got there first."

"Yeah, we won!" Kaboom says.

"What a rip-off," Bethany says.

Ranger Judy ignores them. "First place and the grand prize go to Team Brown Bear." She hands a gold ribbon and a bear charm to Ky. "Congratulations. You've won a brand-new tent."

"Cool. Thanks," Ky says. Bobby whispers something into their ear, and they look surprised. "Okay, if Jimmy doesn't mind."

Bobby whispers something to Jimmy.

"Fine with me," Jimmy says. "Who needs a stinking tent?"

"We've decided to give the tent to Kassy," Ky says. He pushes the tent across the table to me.

"What?" I can't believe it.

Ky nods.

Bobby's cheeks turn pink. "We don't really need another tent."

"Wow—thanks! Really? Are you sure?"

I guess I misjudged the Marino brothers. They're pretty nice guys.

"Team Brown Bear is the best!" Ronny says.

"Yes, we are," Ky says, grinning. They hold up their gold ribbon.

"We have a ribbon too," Gabby says, wiping away a tear and smiling. The ribbon seems to have cheered her up.

"Do you want to pet Freddie?" Crispy asks, holding a tooting Freddie out to Gabby.

"Do you think we can get a ferret?" Gabby asks her brother.

"Maybe." Marco pats Freddie on the head. "Ferrets are pretty cool pets."

"I'll text you my phone number," Ronny says, tapping on her cell phone.

I grimace. If I had a cell phone, then I could text Gabby. She's my friend too.

"Are you gonna try your new tent tonight?" Gabby asks.

"You bet." I nod. I still can't believe I've got a new tent. *What if I get lonely?* I guess I can always crawl back in with my brother, his stinky ferret, my stepsister, her soccer ball, her snoring dog, and our hungry goat. . . . *Whew!* I don't think I'll get *that* lonely.

My first night in the new tent is kind of scary. Lots of weird rustling noises outside keep me awake. But at least I don't have a ferret farting in my face or a hungry goat nibbling on my hair. And tomorrow is Monday—the day we deliver Kiki the travel bug to the National Zoo . . . and my thirteenth birthday.

By the time I wake up, Dad has the new tires on the RV, and everyone else is finishing breakfast.

"Good morning, birthday girl," Dad says. "Better get a move on. We're almost ready to pull out."

"We let you sleep in because it's your birthday," Mari says.

I thought turning thirteen would make me feel different. But I feel pretty much the same as I did yesterday . . . except I'm even more excited for the zoo.

"And I made your favorite—pancakes with strawberries and whipped cream." Mari hands me a plate.

My mouth waters. *Yummy.* I slide down the picnic bench and dish up a stack of pancakes, dump a pile of berries on top, then slather them with a mountain of whipped cream. I take a big bite. *Double yum.* My birthday is off to an excellent start.

"Next stop, the National Zoo," Crispy says. "Freddie can't wait to see the black-footed ferret exhibit. Maybe he'll meet some of his cousins."

I doubt they'll let Freddie into the zoo, but I keep my mouth shut . . . and full of pancakes.

"And Kiki will get her wish." Ronny has the travel bug sitting on the table next to her plate like she's sharing her breakfast with the little koala.

"Come on, kids, load up," Dad says. "We're off to Washington."

I take down my new tent and roll it up.

"Have we got everything?" Mari asks. "Check the campsite before we leave." She's leading Yara on a leash.

Crispy, Ronny, and I circle the campsite, looking for anything we've left behind.

"You've got Kiki, right?" I ask Ronny. "That's the most important thing."

"And Xavier." She bounces the soccer ball off her knee.

"And Freddie," Crispy says, kissing the ferret on the nose.

"And my tent." I hand it to Dad to load in the RV. "We've got everything."

I can't wait to see Washington and go to the zoo, but I'm so tired from our Shenandoah adventure. I fall asleep a few miles down the road and sleep most of the way. When Crispy shakes me, I don't even realize we're already at the zoo.

"We're here!" Ronny yells in my ear.

"Okay, okay," I say, rubbing the sand out of my eyes. "I'm awake."

"Do you have the plastic egg we found Kiki in?" Ronny asks. "We need to put her back inside and find the perfect spot."

I pull Kiki's egg out of my spy vest. "Yup." I hand it to Ronny, and she twists it open.

"We're taking you to the zoo, little travel bug." She kisses Kiki and drops her inside, then puts the two halves of the egg back together and twists it shut again. "Okay, we're ready." She hands the egg back to me, and I stuff it into one of my pockets.

"First stop, the ferret exhibit," Crispy says. "I bet Kiki will like it there."

"I want to take her to see the other bears," Ronny says. "They have pandas and koalas. I think she wants to be with the other koalas."

"Koalas aren't bears," Crispy says. "They're marsupials. Their closest living relatives are wombats."

"Great. More bats." I laugh.

"Wombats aren't bats," Crispy says. "They're more like chubby gophers."

Duh. I was joking.

Two huge lion statues sit on either side of the zoo entrance. Butterflies flutter over an explosion of red and yellow flowers blooming at the front gates. I have butterflies in my stomach too. I'm so excited. What could be better than spending my birthday at the zoo?

Once we're inside the gates, Crispy scopes out the map and makes a beeline for the ferret exhibit.

"Wait. I want to see the pandas," Ronny whines, trailing behind.

"We'll have time to see everything, *mijita*," Mari says, taking Ronny's hand.

The National Zoo is about a million times bigger than our petting zoo back home. They have almost four hundred different species, fifteen of them endangered, including the black-footed ferret.

I read the brochure as we walk. "They have cheetah cubs." *Wow.* There are elephants, tigers, and gorillas . . . With all these

giant animals, I can't believe my brother insists on starting with the ferrets, even if they are endangered. But when Crispy gets an idea into his head, there's no stopping him. I guess we really are related.

The ferrets have both indoor and outdoor enclosures. Without stopping to look at the ferrets playing outside, Crispy dashes inside the ferret house. "They have six new kits," he says as he rounds the corner. He knew about them even before we got to the zoo.

Sure enough, there is a mom ferret with six tiny kits. A plaque near her cage says her name is Potpie and the kits are a month old. I have to admit, they're pretty cute. "*So-o-o* cute," as Gabby would say. Too bad we couldn't bring her to the zoo with us. She'd love these ferret babies.

The kits are chattering, and Freddie answers with chirps.

"What's that noise coming from your backpack?" Dad asks. "You didn't sneak Freddie into the zoo, did you?"

Crispy shrugs. "He wanted to see his cousins."

"I thought I told you to leave him in the RV with Han and Yara. That's why we left the air conditioning on in there." Dad shakes his head and sighs.

"The black-footed ferret is the only ferret native to North America," Crispy says. "In the wild, they live in prairie dog tunnels or the burrows of other animals." At the mention of ferrets, Freddie pokes his head out of my brother's backpack.

"So they live in the ground?" Ronny asks.

Crispy nods . . . and, I swear, so does Freddie.

As we wander from one species to another, I wonder how there can be so many different animals in the world. One sign says there are almost nine million different species on the planet. Human beings are just one species among those millions. Think how lonely humans would be without all the other animals.

"We have to find the koalas," Ronny says.

Ronny is right. We should leave Kiki with the other bears. The koala exhibit makes the most sense.

But first, we stop to see the pandas.

Wow. The giant pandas are roly-poly and playful. They're so fun to watch! I could stay at the panda exhibit all day. But we've got to get Kiki to her koala family.

There are three koalas sitting high up on tree branches, munching on eucalyptus leaves. We watch them through a glass window. Their spoon-shaped noses and fluffy ears are adorable.

"I found the perfect spot," Ronny says. She points to a sign on the wall of the enclosure. She reads the plaque out loud: "*The koala bear is an arboreal herbivorous marsupial native to Australia.*" She looks at Crispy and asks, "What does that mean?"

"*Arboreal* means it lives in trees," Crispy says. "*Herbivorous* means it only eats plants. And *marsupial* means it carries its young in a pouch."

"Cool," Ronny says, gazing up at the koalas.

"Very cool," I say. I wish we had one at our petting zoo.

Ronny puts her hand behind the plaque.

"What are you doing?" I ask.

"There's a little ledge behind the sign. We can put Kiki on it."

I look in the crack behind the plaque. Sure enough, there's a small ledge. "Will her plastic egg fit in there?"

"I think so," Ronny says. I drop the plastic egg into her palm, and she wedges it between the wall and the sign. "Perfect."

"Goodbye, Kiki," I say.

"I wish we could keep her," Ronny says.

"But she's a *travel* bug." Crispy feeds Freddie a piece of popcorn. "She needs to travel."

"And the note in her egg said she wanted to come here to the zoo." I pull the note from my pocket. "We made her wish come true."

"I guess you're right." Ronny taps her phone.

"What are you doing?" I look over her shoulder.

"Telling the geocache app that Kiki made it to the National Zoo." Ronny continues tapping on her phone. *Must be nice.*

After we say goodbye to Kiki, we head to the pavilion for my birthday lunch.

The pavilion is crowded and noisy. Kids are running around everywhere. Dad spots a free table across the room. Getting to it is like swimming upstream.

Whew! We make it through the crowd and to the table. As soon as the server comes over, Dad orders pizza and sodas and hot fudge sundaes for dessert. This is turning out to be a great birthday.

Mari insists on singing "Happy Birthday" to me, and the whole place joins in. Now I wish *I* were a black-footed ferret—then I could crawl into a prairie dog tunnel and disappear. Everyone claps. My cheeks are burning, but I'm smiling at the same time.

Dad reaches into his backpack and pulls out a box wrapped in purple Hello Kitty wrapping paper. He slides it across the table.

"Nice wrapping paper." I realize since I'm thirteen now, I'm a little old for Hello Kitty, but I can't help it. I love her.

I weigh the box in my hand. It's heavier than it looks. *Could it be?* I tear off the wrapping paper, careful not to rip any Hello Kitties. My pulse speeds up. *Holy high tech!*

"Really?" I glance over at Dad.

"It's from your mom and me." He smiles.

Does he mean *Mom* Mom or Mari? I look at Mari.

She's smiling too. "Don't look at me," she says. "It's from your mom and dad."

"Mom got me a cell phone?" I brush a tear from my eye. I can't believe it. I never thought Mom would let me have a phone.

"Don't forget about me," Dad says, laughing. He gets up from his seat, comes around the table, and wraps his arms around me. "Happy birthday, kiddo."

Tears roll down my cheeks, and my chest feels like it might burst open. I hug Dad back, and then Ronny and Crispy join in for one big group hug.

Geocaching, a new tent, strawberry pancakes, Kiki the travel bug, four hundred different species, and, on top of all that, a cell phone . . . This just might be the best birthday ever.

ABOUT THE AUTHOR

KELLY OLIVER is the award-winning, bestselling author of three mysteries series: *The Jessica James Mysteries*, the middle grade *Kassy O'Roarke, Pet Detective Mysteries*, and historical cozies *The Fiona Fig Mysteries*. She is Distinguished Professor of Philosophy at Vanderbilt University. To learn more about Kelly and her books, visit her website with your parent or guardian at www.kellyoliverbooks.com.

If you liked *Kassy O'Roarke, Geocacher* ask your
parents to leave a review of the book. Reviews help
Kassy and her friends keep going on adventures!

CPSIA information can be obtained
at www.ICGtesting.com
Printed in the USA
LVHW042322111220
673919LV00007B/368

9 781643 438214